[the] CONIUM review
vol. 2, no. 1
SPRING 2013

James R. Gapinski
Managing Editor

Uma Sankaram
Senior Editor

Tristan Beach
Associate Editor

Susan Lynch
Associate Editor

Marc Schuster
Guest Editor

Holly Tri
Copy Editor

co·ni·um press

The Conium Review
Vol. 2, No. 1 (Spring 2013)
© 2013 Conium Press
Portland, Oregon

http://www.coniumreview.com

ISBN-10 0982595646
ISBN-13 978-0-9825956-4-0

ISSN 2164-6252

Library of Congress Control Number: 2013900423

All rights to printed materials revert to the individual authors and artists upon publication. No part of this publication may be reproduced or stored in any form without prior consent from the author or artist.

10 9 8 7 6 5 4 3 2 1

This publication is listed in *Duotrope's Digest, Lit List, Every Writer's Resource, The International Directory of Little Magazines & Small Presses, The Writer's Database, The Directory of Poetry Publishers, NewPages, Poets & Writers,* and *Lit Submit.*

Layout: James R. Gapinski
Design: James R. Gapinski and Uma Sankaram
Cover Art: Ivan de Monbrison (ink and acrylic on paper, 12 x 8 inches, Paris, 2011)

Friends & Sponsors

We'd like to thank the supporters of this issue. Without their donations, *The Conium Review* would not be possible.

Ann Gapinski

Mike Gapinski

Bill Rickman

Shirlee Rickman

MARCH 30th 2013

PAULI ! BENESA !

I hope you enjoy my story. It begins on p. 71.

Love,
PATRICK

Bio. is on p. 157

Table of Contents

Flash Fiction

"Of Course I Will Return It," by Shellie Zacharia	/ 1
"Probe," by Tara Deal	/ 2
"Neighbors,'" by Kirby Wright	/ 3
"High Frequency," by J. D. Blair	/ 4-7
"Written," by Jonathan Alston	/ 8-9
"Thirsts," by D. Z. Watt	/ 10-11
"The Greatest Show in the...," by Donald Budge	/ 12-16
"Problems with Schoolboys...," by Ashley Sgro	/ 17

Short Stories

"Orgasm," by Robert Dart	/ 21-30
"A Kidnapping and a...," by Adam Padgett	/ 31-49
"Super Tuschan," by Justin Campbell	/ 50-55
"The Death of an...," by April Rosemary Ehrlich	/ 56-59
"The Best We Can," by William Cass	/ 60-70
"Rheumatic Minutes With...," by Patrick Falconi	/ 71-76

Novelettes

"Never Fight a Crown Fire," by Nick Sansone	/ 79-106
"Like New," by Valerie Cumming	/ 107-129

Poetry

"Shoes," by Don Pomerantz	/ 133
"Niños Perdidos," by Zachariah Middleton	/ 134
"2004 Saturn Vue," by April Salzano	/ 135
"Making Figures in the Ward," by George Seli	/ 136-137
"The House Where Jack...," by William Miller	/ 138-140
"Alex Tells Me He's...," by Brian Baumgart	/ 141
"On the News I Am to Be a...," by Nils Michals	/ 142-145
"Blue Bags," by Thomas Alan Holmes	/ 146
"Grand Jeté," by Steven Ray Smith	/ 147
"Shucking Corn," by David Budbill	/ 148
"*," by Simon Perchik	/ 149
"Take off the Leash," by Sean McPherson	/ 150-151

Biographies

Cover Artist	/ 155
Poets & Writers	/ 155-161
Editors	/ 161-162

Shellie Zacharia
Tara Deal
Kirby Wright
J. D. Blair
Jonathan Alston
D. Z. Watt
Donald Budge
Ashley Sgro

flash·fiction

Of Course I Will Return It
Shellie Zacharia

The woman I want to be lives three houses down. She's a poet and has one of those charming bohemian cottages: white with a bright red door, blooming begonias and marigolds in pots on the porch railing, small white party lights strung in the trees. It looks festive in the evenings, even if she is perhaps reading or writing or baking the cookies she sells at the farmer's market or making pairs from a basket of socks. She rides her sky blue bicycle all over town; she leaves it parked against the mailbox when she's home. Late afternoons she sits on her front porch in a plum wing chair, her legs thrown over the side while she waves a pen in the air as if she were conducting a symphony of bees. Or she plays guitar and sings in a tiny bird voice that stops people passing by—they clap and pause to read her chalk words scribbled on the sidewalk: *green living with laundry lines; plant flowers; smile.* Sometimes a guy with a full beard and a big laugh comes over and he plays guitar and sings too. Once he brought a conga drum. She puts operas on the stereo with the windows open and tosses a Frisbee to her black dog Jake. One day I will take her bicycle.

Probe
Tara Deal

It was the nails that got me: frosted pink, longer than an inch, flicking the wrist corsage of one green-chiffoned alien creature in soft focus. The photograph is my evidence. I look at it and try to remember. But please don't make me relive it. That blur of abduction one night, into the gym, after living under the oppressive atmosphere of the upcoming event, hovering over the entire year. Eyes were glazed, yes, I think that's right. Some of us appeared to have been drugged earlier in the evening.

It's possible that I was so focused on preparation, on stockpiling supplies, and imagining every angle of disaster, that when the event occurred, one spring Friday after dark, I proceeded automatically, following instructions, doing what was necessary, smiling for my friends and relatives. Someone had a camera.

The otherwordly wrist orchid, the small gold chains, and the nails: they prove what happened. I won't try to deny it. Although I can't tell you everything, not now. Just a few details like small scars that remain. Invisible points where vividness was inserted. This is what made me. Made me believe. In another life, an alternate universe, and the possibility of glamour in South Carolina, circa 1985.

Neighbors
Kirby Wright

Is that the message machine talking? No. It's my ex yelling at her boyfriend in their house on the hill. "Goddamn you," she goes, "you horrible man!" She likes him because he takes it the way her mother took it from her father all those years ago in Newport. The boyfriend can't escape because he's on disability and doesn't own a car. Sometimes he wheelchairs into their backyard, throws tangerines that roll onto my patio. Yesterday one hit the roof. I'd toss them back, but that would start a war. "Where the hell are you?" my ex calls.

High Frequency
J. D. Blair

Randall Tims returned from the dentist with several new fillings, and that night as he lay in bed in the quiet of a clear November night, his teeth began receiving radio broadcasts. He believed that the music was coming from the neighbor girl who kept her windows open and had her radio too loud when in fact what he heard was coming from his left molar. He turned over and went to sleep to Classic Rock 105. The next night when Randall went to bed he slept easily at first but after a few hours woke with Brahms Second Symphony ringing in his ears. His right bicuspid was picking up a broadcast out of Salt Lake City and Randall tossed and turned until he finally dropped off to sleep listening to Starlight Symphonies from KQEL.

Over several weeks Tims' mouth picked up programming from a wide range of formats: everything from rock to classical and oldies, folk and talk. One night his first bicuspid engaged in a heated exchange with a wisdom tooth over the merits of back-channel diplomacy in the Middle East. He slept little that night, frustrated that he couldn't take part in the discussion. On another night he tossed and turned when a pirate radio station off the coast of Mexico played every top ten rock and roll oldie between 1956 and 1965. Tims claimed that a lateral incisor and a cuspid were actually vibrating during the entire musical countdown.

When Randall went in for his next dental checkup he told his dentist that his mouth was picking up radio signals and the dentist said Randall was probably hallucinating.

"You would have to have a very large antenna to pick up such a wide range of programming," said the dentist.

The dentist told Randall to try rearranging the furniture in his bedroom which he did but that only increased the volume of the broadcasts that now included satellite programming; Tims was getting shock jocks ranting in his ear at all hours of the night, but commercial free.

Randall returned to the dentist who replaced the fillings. He reduced the amount of metal in the amalgam and sent Tims on his way. Tims slept well for a few weeks until the night he started picking up strange coded messages bombarding his wisdom teeth. He was listening in on top-secret exchanges between Washington and the United Arab Emerites.

"Helium balloons stretched thin above arid oases," said the UAE.

"Knicks 94, Raptors 88," answered Washington.

For an entire month Tims was barraged with ciphers from every corner of the world.

"Winter in Norway is balmy," sent NATO headquarters.

"Klaatu Verada Nikto," responded Area 51.

When his wisdom teeth weren't picking up ciphers his lower bicuspids were taking shout-outs from truckers on the interstate.

"This is Big Dog from Denver, c'mon back."

"Big Dog this is Top Gun on a heading out of Tucson. What are you hauling, c'mon back?"

"Spuds from Idaho," responded Big Dog.

Top Gun was carrying a load of illegal aliens out of Arizona.

One night an upper bicuspid began beeping when it received an SOS call from a thirty-foot sloop in trouble off the coast of Newfoundland. The boat was sending out an alert signal that was being boosted by the boat's mast. Randall called the Coast Guard who located the boat, towed it to safety and rescued the two people on board.

After several months Tims got into a routine of listening to his teeth each night and discovered that by positioning his jaw just right on the pillow and moving his teeth in certain ways he could surf the airwaves and change stations. He became adept at listening for announcements of the time allowing him to wake himself each morning without an alarm clock.

Randall became accustomed to his mouth's receptions but soon was frustrated that it wasn't enough; he wanted broadband and on his next checkup instructed the dentist to give him a full set of braces. The dentist balked saying it wasn't necessary but Tims insisted and the dentist complied. Today Randall's mouth is capable of picking up audio signals from both radio and television worldwide, and he is working on a technique that will allow him to listen in stereo.

Written
Jonathan Alston

Len wrote me a letter on handmade yellow parchment. Dense. Short. Green script grew over the page uncut. It was simple: I miss you, I love you. We missed and loved each other every day. Sometimes more.

They were words, expressions that, over time, bled into the cracks in the paper. I read her letter again. I miss you. I tried to peel the green ink from the page, hoping to find hidden letters beneath. But the ink was dry, fused to the fibers. I thought perhaps between words—the letters themselves— were smaller, truer letters, other sentences I had not seen. Missing F's, P's, and S's. A few vowels filling in. Magnifying glasses proved useless; I attempted a microscope. It only exposed the paper threads and ink. Where were those letters? Against my fingers, running them over her sentences, I felt them; somewhere mixed with the yellow and green, and brown and white wood bits disrupting the clean sheet.

Days wasted, dissecting. I cut out each word, laying the pieces on a black table, rearranging their order, writing her letter anew. Each composition produced the same lines: I miss you, I love you. That is not what she meant. There was more.

My brother offered access to an electron microscope, down to the very atoms themselves to expose the hidden letters. I blinked only between specimens. But her green words melted into inky fractals discharged to blind from an escape. I fell into those words. Meaning lost, every syllable beyond distinction; letters twisted, broke, folded over, a mass plait ripped from her prose.

She hid her letters well. Deep. They lived on the table. I could not look at them. But I heard them. I felt them with each passing: I love you. Her voice taunting. Faint green laughter popped out of words, precise elocutions gouging my ears.

It became too much, her squawk echoed through my bones. But I could not touch those words; the table suffered.

It burned.

Slow.

Hot.

Eating sentences, taking away her hidden letters.

Thirsts
D. Z. Watt

Don't pass by the oasis without pausing to drink. That's what his mother used to say. But for Albert, a child of city streets with fountains, the expression seemed the arcane idea of a woman whose need for love he only saw in maternal terms.

Inspecting the grey-specked stubble on his face, he decided to let it go today and got in the shower, a once-clear plastic box now milky with soap splashes, its corners filled with slimy black he'd gradually come to unnotice.

On the bus to work, he nodded to some regulars, trying not to stare at the gorgeous young man in the middle of the back seat and sat instead next to a new face. Not because of her perky forty-something look, *obviously*. But because she was thin and he'd have more room — having learned to avoid fat people or macho guys with legs spread wide into his half of the seat.

At once he was aware that she was aware of him. And he stiffened against being social. Not that he disliked women, socially. But he'd grown cautious of misleading them, by the nods and smiles that might confirm attraction, into thinking he was interested in *that* way. And that, unfortunately, was the way they often seemed to look at hi — when he was affable. While, ironically, of course, he was interested in the lad back there, but from the way the boy was dressed Albert suspected they shared nothing social.

The twenty-three blocks to work he feigned indifference to her sidelong and even bold straightforward looks, which made him feel like a striptease.

So it was a relief to see his office building coming up next. And as he grasped the bar to pull himself up, the young man from the back leaned across him and said, "Mum, this is our stop."

The Greatest Show in the Universe
Donald Budge

In a jade theater inside the moon, the greatest show in the universe plays.

Where the most loving man in the world dies and is reborn every single night in front of an audience of no one. He dies because he has no one to love. He comes back because he knows there could be. Slowly, he has been perfecting his performance over centuries that fall off time like wrinkled leaves. He is not a patient man. But sometimes life makes you patient.

Before there was wind or sound, he had the good fortune to love someone completely. Now he's merely an ember of an old flame. But he's been preparing his hearth for some time now. This is his comeback.

One day a little girl with blueberry eyes and a watermelon soul strolls into the theater carrying a stuffed frog with a jewel in its belly. She isn't lost. But this isn't where she was going either. She sits in the second row, and the red curtains melt into liquid velvet, pouring onto the floor and tickling her alabaster ankles.

The man appears on stage in all of his unwavering splendor. His cummerbund is neatly pressed. His blue blazer is well cut. He takes off his top hat and places it on the ground, where it erupts into violet flames.

She does not smile.

But surely when he unveils the ceiling to be a skylight, and the majestic glow of the Earth pours in, she will be impressed. After all, it took him nearly three hundred years to figure out how to make glass from moon rock. With a snap of his fingers, the ceiling collapses to reveal the glory of the Earth illuminating him and the stage.

The man puts on a spectacular show, dancing in his shimmering shoes. The doves are on cue. The fire sings and roars with his steps. His entire body is life. He tames a meteor and rides it around the stage. He is inspiration in a tuxedo.

She doesn't clap.

Alright. Tough crowd tonight. No matter. He hasn't even begun. The second act will melt that icy demeanor.

Taking his time, the man picks the brightest red star from the sky, cuts it open, and pours its celestial nectar and a pinch of brown sugar into his pet black hole.

With one swift motion, the man takes out a crystal cello with continents and oceans swirling inside. When he plays, disasters stir. Seven volcanos erupt when the C chord is plucked. An ice age triggers with the next. Civilizations rise and fall in his crescendo. The cello begins to crack, as the entire drama of life plays in his song. Waves of light-stained music leak out of its crystal crevices, filling the auditorium with dancing colors and clouds. Now the girl rests on a fluffy watermelon cloud, as the aurora borealis washes over her, each wave cooing to the man's soaring melodies. The clouds turn into dancers who dive into the brilliant vermillion water below. They rise with the beat. The greens and yellows of the northern lights bend and shout over the girl's body, hardening into bracelets and earrings designed only for her.

She yawns.

The man tries to keep his composure. Does she not understand what's happening? Is she frightened? Confused? It doesn't matter. All this paled in comparison to what was coming next. It was time for the finale. Even she would be moved by what was about to happen.

He plunges his arm into the flaming top hat, and pulls out what was cooking inside the black hole. It's not worth discussing how much time he took to figure that out. A ball of light rests in his hands. The air around him shivers in ecstasy. He knows he doesn't have much time left. Opening his mouth wide, he swallows the glimmering sphere. The light in his eyes retreats to some unknown shore. He collapses onto the stage, dead. The girl doesn't know that he comes back. She holds her frog so tight that the jewel pops out of his left eye.

Just like the cello, cracks appear in the man's body, and the universe spills out of him. All of his love pours out, recreating the universe.

Stars are born and collapse upon themselves, releasing billowing burgundy clouds that smell of cinnamon. Wild nebulas shoot past her riding the wave of creation. Swirling galaxies explode in a spectacular display that only lasts for a few seconds, but fits in an eternity of magic.

As the fabric of the universe begins to settle, the man snaps back to life. Slowly, but surely, he returns. First, his hands begin moving. Then his legs. Then his eyes open. Finally, he rises.

The girl cries.

The man is shocked. Visions of dapper crowds cheering vanish. In his thousands of years, he never imagined his audience crying.

Nervously he looks around, unsure what to do. Until he notices the strange jewel resting by his feet. The jewel he gave his daughter so many years ago. My how she's grown. She's standing next to him, her blueberry eyes begin to water.

"You didn't have to do all that. I love you because you're my dad."

She hugs him. He cries. He laughs.

Over these hundreds of years alone, even he forgot.

It's stupid. It's silly. It's the greatest show in the universe.

Problems with Schoolboys on Trains
Ashley Sgro

There's the approaching light. The train whistle and open car door. I'm stepping into the vestibule. Turning to my right to walk down the stairs of the fifth car. Looking for an empty seat and—

Oh, there's that foot again. That foot with a shoe on it. Dark brown and dull. Sole up against the side of the blue train seat. There's a leg too. A leg wrapped in bone-colored cotton. A foot, a leg, and (oh, yes) a knee. Upright and pointed at its owner's head.

That foot/leg/knee combo connects to form a line. A sturdy line. A big line graph line cutting across the aisle.

And, I know, there has to be another leg. This one's like a pole.

So his pole leg: planted. And his line graph leg: static. Like a stiff flag. A territorial flag. Unwavering. Smug.

(short)stories

Robert Dart
Adam Padgett
Justin Campbell
April Rosemary Ehrlich
William Cass
Patrick Falconi

Orgasm
Robert Dart

The traffic had abated. The air was dry, warm, unsettling. My friend Veronica was just telling me about the orgasm she had purchased two days prior.

"You'll never believe it," she said. "This orgasm is unlike anything you've ever seen."

I took a sip of coffee. I was excited for Veronica. I valued our friendship and wanted to prompt her with the best kind of questions, like good friends and talk-show hosts do.

"What do you mean?" I asked.

"Think of an orgasm," she said, and I thought of one. "Now completely erase it from your mind because this orgasm is unlike any other."

"I'm having a tough time doing that," I said. It was no longer morning. It was full daytime now and my legs were getting sticky; I was wishing I had shorts on instead of jeans. "I mean," I said. Veronica looked impatient. I must not have been giving her the right opportunity to explain. "Well, what's it like?" I asked.

"You want me to tell you what an orgasm is like?" asked Veronica, now giving me her full attention.

"Not any orgasm. This one you just purchased. Like how is it different?"

"Oh, you want me to tell you how this orgasm is different?"

"Exactly," I said, and drank more coffee.

"You should have just said so. You know how an orgasm…" here Veronica's eyes went wide, she extended her arms—"an orgasm is like fireworks"—her hands opened, now making a giant, seated Y—"or like maybe scratching an itch until the itch becomes, like, something else entirely. Like a nice cold drink from one of those bars with the fancy ice-cubes."

"Yes," I said, "it could be put in those terms."

"Well I'm glad you agree. This orgasm, to the contrary, is more like eating fifty jalapeno poppers and then competing in the Henley Royal Regatta."

"I see."

"Or you could say it's akin to eating a gram of marijuana butter before taking your Step Two medical examinations — and you know all of the answers! Every one of them. You ace those examinations. Otherwise the effects of the marijuana butter are quite present."

"That is," I said, "very different from any of my orgasms."

"I know it is," said Veronica. "That's why I brought up this subject!" She was very animated now, excited to be telling her story.

"One time my girlfriend," I said, "took her index finger and…"

"And what was that like?"

"Rather like eating a bowl full of oat bran and some good strong coffee for breakfast," I said. I thought to take another sip of coffee but it was all gone now.

"That isn't what I'm talking about," Veronica said. "What girlfriend?" She furrowed her eyebrows at me, then relaxed. "Oh, right, no. How stupid of me. Yes. Your girlfriend. Please continue."

"I was just saying, once she took her index finger and — you know it was very unexpected. I hadn't said anything —"

"Right, no, yes. No, not at all. That isn't what I'm getting at." Veronica had only ordered a small coffee, mine a large, but she still wasn't finished. "Have you ever given blood?" she asked.

"Of course," I said. "In high school we all gave blood."

Veronica tilted her head wistfully. "One does, yes. We gave some blood. Did you ever wonder," she asked, "where it all went?"

"It went into a blood bank."

"A blood bank! How stupid. Anyway," she said, "it's like you've just given blood and now this sexy blonde woman with a really nice body, she's naked, has come to give you a lap dance. But instead of a lap dance, she gives you a handmade greeting card. You know, she made it herself. And it's a really nice, bonded card, baby blue, and she's folded it into a wonderful origami."

"What shape is it?"

"I told you, she has a nice body."

"No, what's the origami?"

"That's just it. It's an origami woman, blonde, nude, with a really nice body. And she has a card."

"And that card's a girl too?"

"No, that card is a card. How can a card be a girl?"

I didn't know. I looked across the street, where people were walking in and out of a Seven-Eleven.

"You should just come over and see it," she said. "Come on." She downed the rest of her coffee and tossed the cup into a waste-bin.

It was an easy stroll over to Veronica's place. Pine trees had littered pine needles all over the sidewalk.

"There she is," she said, opening the door. I was wondering why orgasms, like sailing vessels, were always referred to in the feminine. "Isn't she a beaut?" she said. And she was, there was no denying her that, sitting Indian-style at Veronica's desk, attending to her social media.

She was one of these red colored orgasms, or at least she was red at this particular moment. She closed her window and looked at us, blank and poised.

"Hello," I said. Then I turned to Veronica. "Say," I said. "Could I borrow this orgasm sometime?"

"Sorry," said Veronica.

"Not today or anything."

"Sorry," said Veronica. "I'd love to loan you my orgasm, but I'm afraid I just can't. It's impossible, sorry." Then

Veronica walked over to her orgasm. "Well," she said, and made introductions.

She shook my hand very politely, sitting there with fantastic posture. It was clear to me this orgasm had nothing in her past to be ashamed of, and little fear for the future. It made me a little uneasy, and that made me think of how Veronica had described her, and it all started to make some semblance of sense.

"What have you been up to all day?" I asked her.

"Oh, nothing much. As you can see from my Twitter account." She then enlarged the window from the bottom of her screen, and I peered over her shoulder to see. The orgasm's Twitter account had many followers.

The page was filled with nothing much, just as she'd said, in the following manner:

    Orgasm @orgasm   1h
    Nothing much

    Orgasm @orgasm   2h
    Nothing much

    Orgasm @orgasm   3h
    Nothing much

"Well that's it," said Veronica, slipping her arms back into her coat.

"What do you mean?" I said.

"I thought we might put together this puzzle," said the orgasm and lifted up the puzzle box to show us. It was a rainbow sky with birds of different shapes and sizes. It looked to be a difficult one; it looked like a lot of fun.

"No time for puzzles," said Veronica, "this was just a quick introduction." The orgasm looked sad and I must have looked sad too. Veronica was neglecting this orgasm horribly. And anyway, an orgasm is for two people, not one. "I've got to get my haircut in a moment and Louis here, I'm sure, has his own matters to deal with," she said.

Back outside I resolved to steal this orgasm away from Veronica, or at least to apply my best efforts for an extended period of time towards stealing her. I sat up all night thinking it over.

At around six the next evening I stopped by old Veronica's place with a premium bottle of Japanese whiskey. "Look here," I said, "let's have a glass of this premium Japanese whiskey and see where that leads us."

"Oh look," said Veronica, "so nice to see you and thank you for dropping by." Veronica was sitting on her couch, painting her toenails. The orgasm was doing same. It had turned blue, a lovely cerulean shade.

"My orgasm and I have time for one quick drink," she said. "Then I'm going to kick you out, sorry."

"What have you got planned?" I asked. The orgasm looked unhappy. I think she was unhappy.

"It's rude of you to ask, isn't it, but I'll tell you, we're having a makeup party." She motioned to a pile of lipsticks, little round containers and big tall square ones, an enormous supply of cosmetics. "Boys aren't invited to makeup parties."

"But—"

"Louis, if you attend the makeup party, I'll no longer see you in the masculine light you've basked in over the years; it would be terribly damaging; in several moments you would set fire to all the evidence you've accumulated showing you're a man who does man things, etcetera."

I looked at the orgasm to see if she agreed with this assessment. It was hard to say; she just looked at me blankly and then back at her toes. She was painting them white. It went well with the blue.

Veronica got up and poured us all drinks. We were sitting on the floor listening to The Carpenters.

"So," I said, turning to the orgasm, "how do you like the new digs?"

"It's nice here," she said, "quiet and clean."

"And are you excited about this makeup party?"

"I don't know. I've never made up before."

I looked down into my scotch, halfway gone. The Carpenters were making me feel pleasant. "I'm a fan of making up," I said. "I sincerely hope it doesn't make me unmanly."

"I don't think so," said the orgasm.

"Well," said Veronica, "there are two opinions about that."

"I never wear any makeup but I'm always making up, you know."

"Ha, ha," said Veronica. She was making angry eyes at me. I actually liked her angry eyes.

"Why is it women are always making up with women and never with men?" I asked.

"Because you are a horrible sexist pig," said Veronica.

"I think that's uncalled for, old friend."

"Old friend? Ha! You come around now that you've heard about my orgasm, but where were you when I was lonely, when I hadn't bought one yet?"

"I was only just up the street," I said.

"You never came to my house with a bottle of whiskey in those days."

"I Gchatted you. How often did I send you a Gchat?"

"That's only because you hated your job and because you're a lazy sexist pig."

"Well," I said, "I still hate my job."

"And you're still sexist. Stop looking at my orgasm like that."

"I can't help it. She's naked and pretty."

"Go put on some clothes," said Veronica to her orgasm. The orgasm hesitated a moment, Veronica repeated herself, and then the orgasm got up and went into the bedroom.

I told Veronica she shouldn't speak to her orgasm like that.

"I should never have informed you of my orgasm," she said.

"Perhaps not," I said.

Veronica drank her whiskey. I stared off, and we were silent for a moment. Karen Carpenter was asking the man with the sad guitar if he remembered, expressing her strong desire for his return. The orgasm came back into our circle wearing a disheveled party dress. It looked as though she had put the dress on, then taken it halfway off, then rolled around on the floor for seven or eight minutes.

"Strumpet!" shouted Veronica. "Can't you even put a dress on right? And did I say put on my sexy party dress? Go back in there and put on my frumpy jeans, the ones in the dirty clothes pile, and a sweatshirt, please and thank you."

"Please excuse Veronica," I said, "from the way she speaks, I think you're probably her first orgasm; she doesn't know how to act."

"Well nobody ever left one on my doorstep," said Veronica.

"No need to change," I said, "here let me just put that on right for you."

"Sit down," said Veronica. "I'll fix it."

"Veronica," I said, "from the looks of it you're jealous of your own orgasm."

Instead of fixing the dress, Veronica unplugged the record player and shook her glass in my face. "Don't you tell me how to raise my orgasm," she said. "At least I don't let mine run around the city unattended, like a wild dog, chasing cars and putting its paws all over pedestrians. At least mine is housebroken. At least mine doesn't have worms and rickets from sleeping under bridges and in vacant lots and wherever else it rolls its dirty hide at night—"

"—Rickets? I dewormed her last February—"

"No wonder you covet my orgasm," she said. "Seeing how badly you've screwed up your own."

She was right, in part; I hadn't seen my orgasm for a fortnight. I'm not sure what she'd got up to. Here was the thing about Veronica. She was always right. There was a time when I first met her, and we would sit in a coffee shop that resembled very much a poorly stocked library for adolescents. This coffee shop had orange carpet, harsh lighting, and a lot of open space that ought to have been filled with additional tables, but was not. We never drank any coffee in those days. In those days I would tell Veronica half-truths with great sincerity and pretend that I knew everything, and she would pretend with great sincerity to believe me. Even then, however, I knew that Veronica actually knew everything. I was only beginning to understand—it was a mere glimmer inside of me—my actual strength, which was ignorance. It was the seed of our friendship and also a clear sign of things to come. We had an expiration date.

After that date we switched places and Veronica began telling me about things while I took a breather and asked good questions. Now I was prompted to take back my chair and tell Veronica about all the things I didn't know, like in the old days. The first item on my list was Veronica's orgasm.

"First of all," I said, "your orgasm doesn't like The Carpenters, that much is clear. You only think she does. Second, don't put your orgasm in sweats. Let her wear the crooked party dress if she wants. Third, an orgasm doesn't like discipline in most cases. In most cases you ought to just give your orgasm a key; she might need to get out of the apartment sometimes; she might even buy you groceries if you give her the freedom to do so. She doesn't care about makeup either. You should know, you're ruining your orgasm."

As I was finishing my speech, Veronica was taking my glass away and showing me, with great insistence, where the door was. Soon thereafter I was standing outside in the cool evening, short of one fancy whiskey bottle.

I walked home slowly, whistling a happy tune. My orgasm was sleeping on the couch; she'd let herself in and knew where breakfast could be found. I watched her twitching in her sleep. Maybe she was chasing squirrels. I laid down on the mattress and tried to fall asleep myself.

The next day I got a Gchat from Veronica.

Veronica: hi
me: hello. sorry about last night
Veronica: dont be sorry. this is veronicas orgasm
me: oh, did she give you her password?
Veronica: i figured it out. so whats up?
me: nothing much. slow day
Veronica: yeah i hear ya

I looked at my spreadsheet for a moment, then back at my Gmail window. I had so many questions. I was thinking about her little white toenails, what color her feet were at present, what she had done with that crooked party dress. Before I could ask her any of those things, the orgasm wrote: "so do you want to meet me at Baskin Robbins?"

I did, and there we met.

What Veronica had said was true. It was a euphoric and gut-wrenching experience, and after a while I felt as though I'd done something special, against all odds, and at great price. At Baskin Robbins the orgasm wanted an eating contest, so that's what we had, and after that, wind-sprints on the sidewalk. So I did that too, and felt sick, until the sickness became something different and I just wanted to get it over with, quick. Then I noticed how fast I was running.

This orgasm had a lot of imagination. I don't know how but we soon found ourselves on an old battleship that had been outfitted for a party excursion. Of course we hit a storm. It was an old ship and it couldn't sit still through a storm—it pitched back and forth, the ground slipped out from under us, the DJ had to put away all his equipment, and the only music was old cassette tapes played over the PA system. Little vomit baggies appeared in the hallways, and the only way to get through it was to drink Tequila shots until the inner ear somehow accepted these conditions. And it worked! Then we were perfectly balanced and poised while the other guests slammed against the walls, vomiting in their hands.

As soon as we were back on dry land, the orgasm demanded a headstand, so I tried that out, falling over a bunch. Then I was tired. She wanted to visit the dentist, but I had no interest in that.

In truth I was soon missing my old orgasm. But who knows where she was. We hadn't actually spoken in some time; we seemed to keep different hours. We were strolling by the coffee shop and I wasn't sure whether I should drop the orgasm off at Veronica's or take her back to my place; I was quite tired and I don't think this one ever slept.

Then we passed Veronica and my old shaggy O., enjoying the twilight, reading trashy novels. Or maybe they were good novels, I'm not sure.

No, it was a book of short stories.

Veronica put hers down. "Henry, I hate these endings," she said.

A Kidnapping and a Church Van
Adam Padgett

I've been doing a lot of thinking about honesty lately. I have been quite the liar, but often the lies are out of love, the need to protect something precious. If my lies have hurt my former wife, then I am sorry. If they have hurt or will hurt my child, then I am sorry. I can only tell them later that my intentions have only been sincere and earnest.

I look at my child now. He stands outside my car, the window down and the empty square frames his head as though in a picture. His long brown hair hides his eyebrows neatly like drapes and he stares at me with large, dark eyes. The earnest kind. I tell him that we are going on a trip just the two of us. This is not the lie. The lie comes after the question he will undoubtedly ask. Elliot pulls open the passenger door and the door opens slow and heavy. Elliot is eight years old. He throws his bag in and sits beside me. He asks me if he's supposed to sit in the back. I tell him no. I tell him that today he gets to sit up front. He asks me if his mother is going on the trip. His already large eyes open a little wider. I tell him that she isn't and his eyes dim and look straight ahead. He asks me why, and I tell him it's because she has to work. This is the lie. This is the lie that will bloom, spread and generate more lies, and those lies will be more convoluted than the ones before. But for now, I've told the one. I can manage one mistruth and it will do for the time being.

I am taking him away from his home and away from his mother without her knowing. It feels strange, nearly criminal. A confluence of rights and wrongs that, when I think about it, makes me close my eyes and remember the sincerity. The intention. That what I am doing is out of love and protection. I've done a good amount of praying on what I have done. And I am reassured that my intentions are earnest.

In the back of the car, tucked between the backseat and my seat, is a piece of luggage I bought from a Wal-Mart, filled with clothes for Elliot I bought from the same Wal-Mart. We pull away from the Elementary School and find the interstate, knowing I only have a few hours to drive without police cars checking for my make and model. We get on I-85 and drive toward Charlotte. We drive for nearly an hour with little to no conversation. I reach over and attempt to tousle Elliot's hair and he pulls back as though irritated. I return my hand to the steering wheel and listen to the radio. It's an oldies station and Springsteen is on. I reach over and turn the volume up three subtle notches. He sings, "Held up without a gun, held up without a gun."

"I'm hungry," Elliot says to me. I reach again and turn the volume back down.

"Okay," I say.

I drive, reading the blue road signs. I see one with a Cracker Barrel and take the next exit. We pull into the restaurant and are seated with a waitress that calls me "Hun" and calls Elliot "Honey." Elliot orders a burger and I make him replace the French fries with the green bean casserole. Boy's got to eat his greens, I suppose. After we eat, we both go to the rest room. I check my cell phone for the last time.

I have been in correspondence with a pastor. We first met in an online discussion board several months ago. We exchanged numbers and now the plan is to meet in Charlotte this evening. He is riding with three other evangelist-types who are traveling the south, spreading the word of the impending rapture (Judgment Day, End of Times, whatever you'd like), set to befall on the world in a matter of weeks. I told him of my interest to spread the word. Told him there was no calling higher. I did not tell him I planned to take my child in the manner in which I have. Figured it'd be counterproductive.

I stand in one stall, Elliot stands in the other. I open my phone and there are nine missed calls. All from my ex-wife. I clear the missed calls and confirm one last time with the pastor via text. Once sent, I urinate in the toilet and drop the phone in the water and flush. The phone doesn't go down, but the yellow does. By the time I am done, Elliot has washed his hands and is waiting on me. I wash mine and ask him if he is ready to go. He looks at me and says that he is.

. . .

I leave my car at a light rail station in Charlotte. We ride the only line to downtown. We meet the pastor on the corner of 4th and College Street. The van is large and all white, though it does have "Mason County Baptist" written in a cursive font across the side. The pastor leans against the van parked on the street wearing a tie and short-sleeved shirt. Sunglasses hiding his eyes from the setting sun. Once close enough to say hello, I realize the pastor is a younger man, younger than me by probably several years. A thick sweeping of black hair is oiled and combed neatly to the side. He smells of his hair product.

As we greet each other on the street curb, he shakes my hand and calls me "brother" and invites me onboard. I look at Elliot and tell him to go on and he does. We squeeze between the seats and the tangle of seatbelts hanging. We find our seats in the back of the van. The model appears newer, and as the air conditioning blows, I can smell clean plastic blast through the ducts. Their church must've been nice. Must've had lots of members and lots of support—something I valued from the pastor, from these people I just met. I buckle by seatbelt and make sure Elliot does the same. Each head turns toward us. Each smiling, each asking how we are doing and each asking for our story.

・ ・ ・

We've been traveling with the team for nearly a week now. Six of us ride—five adults and one child. The others are members of the Mason County Baptist Church, each have quit their jobs, quit their identities for this journey. We stop at gas stations, city parks, and pass out tracts and spread the word. We save souls. That is the hope at least. Before this, I had an apartment. I drove a 1990 Ford Taurus. A green one. The paint: cracked and chipped. I lived alone. My son, with his Jewish mother who refused to convert Elliot or herself to Christianity. The reason she left. The reason I found myself alone.

The pastor pulls into a gas station. I am unsure of what town we're in, but I know that we're somewhere in South Carolina. The air feels different than it did in North Carolina. A trick of the mind, I figure. But the new air feels just like that, new, and there is relief in the newness. We unbuckle while the pastor gives us a speech about being warriors for the Lord, our collective chests swelling with that sense of purpose and belonging. Once the speech is over, we exit into the parking lot, papers in hands. Doing what we are meant to do, doing what God has sent us here to do. Bits of glass and loose pavement crumble under our tennis shoes as Elliot and I walk across the blacktop, finding a spot, near the front door, in the shade. I offer, but Elliot does not hold my hand. After a few minutes in the shade, sweat forms over my brow and under my arms. The door to the icebox is open and the icebox holds no ice. Rust from a gutter stains the gray concrete swirls of orange and red and the stain looks very much like a river. I notice that there are more Hispanic patrons than any other ethnicity. I gently tug at the wooden cross resting on my chest. A habit I've picked up.

The plan is to greet people as they go in and out of the convenience store. I've had to train myself to be extroverted. To think of myself as not a social nuisance, but as a Godly soldier. I stand with feet slightly apart, chest puffed in a way that should exude friendly confidence and not eager aggression. I ask Elliot to put his game away and I hand him two paper tracts so that he'll feel like a part of the team. He puts his game away, as I've asked, and holds the paper between his stubby fingers. A woman approaches and I smile, extending my hand with the small pamphlet of paper that reads, "It's Not Too Late" printed on the front. The woman, dark-skinned and dumpily shaped, smiles back and takes the tract from my hand and walks inside the store. I tell Elliot that it's as simple as that. The next woman—an older woman, probably Mexican—approaches, he hands her a tract and she smiles like the one before did and walks inside the store.

We do this for several minutes, even after the van has long been refueled. Elliot hands out his last paper tract and pulls his video game from his pocket. I hand him two more and he tells me that he doesn't want to any more. I tell him to do it for Jesus and attempt to take away his game. Our stubby fingers aren't much for coordination and in our struggle, the game falls from our hands and breaks in two parts. He looks at the pieces on the ground and then at me and back at the ground. Water swells in his eyes and he begins to cry an angry cry. Tells me that he hates me. I try to console him, to tell him that we are doing Jesus' work, but he only cries louder and harsher and says that he hates me and hates Jesus.

Only four weeks until the rapture and I wish that he wouldn't say such things.

. . .

I was in love with my wife and sometimes I think that I am still in love with her. When I look at our child I see her. I see her in his eyes that are large and dark and framed with long lashes. The most heartbreaking thing I've ever done is have a child. To love something more than you can love anything only to have it reject and deny reciprocation with only a look of large round eyes.

Georgia is only an hour or so away and the van drives down the interstate, rhythmic thumps from the tires and pavement have put Elliot asleep and I want him to stay that way. I reach over and put my arm round his shoulders and he doesn't flinch or move, only sleeps. Wet from the recent cry still on his cheeks.

The church deposits money in the pastor's checking account on a weekly basis. We don't eat until the pastor can afford to, until he gives us money. Though, I suspect that Hank—the rich fat man who always sits in the front passenger seat—has plenty of money saved up and spends it frequently and in secret. Often I'll see smudges of grease in the corners of his mouth or below his mustache when we haven't eaten for hours. Maybe he just has poor hygiene. Regardless, I've decided that I don't prefer Hank's company and haven't bothered to get to know him.

We only stay in hotels when we can afford it, and today we can. The sun edges down past the flat, marshy horizon. We are somewhere near the coast. We unload the van. The pastor gives me a hundred dollars in cash and I arrange a room with twin beds for Elliot and me. The hotel isn't particularly nice, but it has a large lobby and modest swimming pool that I don't think gets cleaned very often. Elliot and I get our own room because I am the only one with a child on the trip. We drop our belongings on the carpeted floor and Elliot lays on his bed, reading a comic book I bought for him at a used bookstore. He hasn't talked to me in two days. I've decided to wait for him to come around. His eyes appear dead, emotionless as they peruse the images and text.

I leave Elliot in the room as the group reconvenes in the hotel lobby. The pastor says that he has run out of tracts and, in the morning, he will drive to a Kinko's to print off some more. The pastor tells us that this will be a good time to strengthen the group's relationship. To bond. To talk about Jesus and to refuel our spiritual tanks.

In the hotel lobby, we've pulled three circular tables together so that we all can sit around and talk about Jesus and our testimonies. For a while no one speaks. We all stare at each other. I look up and make eye contact with Jeffery, the sole black person on the crusade, and he smiles at me and I smile back. We share an awkward moment and then Jeffery clears his throat and starts talking. He addresses the group and finally goes into a personal story. He confesses that he used to have a taste for the whores and other pleasures of the flesh before he was saved.

As he tells his story of debauchery, his eyes look briefly at everyone and he pauses.

"It's okay," the pastor says. He leans back, uncrosses and recrosses his legs and smiles—I think he whitens his teeth. "The bell of Jesus' message rings the clearest through honesty."

Jeffery runs a hand through his trimmed carpet of gray hair covering his scalp and says, "okay." And continues with his story. He steers clear of the gory details but is honest and candid with the group. Jeffery, a black man and of the nicest people I've ever met. He has a lazy eye, but I think he earns people's trust because of it. I have a hard time imagining his years of late-night rendezvous with strange women whom he kept from his wife. He is single now, he tells the group, but he loves talking about Jesus and the Bible, whether it be with friends or strangers at a gas station. "Don't make no matter who it is," he says, and the group chuckles awkwardly.

After Jeffery's story, we sit in another silence. Hank speaks up. He tells the group of his gambling problem and his addiction to pornography. Marry-Ellen, the only woman in the group, tells us of how she used to be an atheist until the car accident that changed her life. She shows us the sloppy scar carved under the tender part of her arm, just past her armpit. These stories, like badges of honor. A ticket you've earned to show that you are worthy of being a part of this all-important crusade. Like earning a purple heart in order to ride a purple-hearts-only ride.

When it becomes my turn, I speak briefly on my former drinking problem and prescription drug problem and how I quit after I found Jesus. I tell the group that Cognac was my favorite. I tell them that as my ex-wife, Rachel, pushed Elliot out and into this world, I was busy vomiting all I was worth into the parking lot of a Hooters. And that a nice young lady named Jessica rubbed my back during. I got some on her white tennis shoes and socks. But that's where the telling stopped. I leave out some of the more indigestible bits. Like I don't tell them that my former wife is a Jew who refused to convert. I don't tell them how she told me to go to hell and then left me, taking my son away. I don't tell them how I kidnapped Elliot and that he is probably on some kind of missing persons list. I leave a lot out of my story but figure that details are on a need-to-know kind of basis.

■ ■ ■

The group session has long been over and now I stand and lean, alone, on the slightly rusted railing outside our hotel room, staring at the dirty swimming pool that reflects green against the white concrete. I see Mary-Ellen on the other side of the pool, leaning on her rail. She looks up, and I can't tell if she's looking at me or merely staring off. I lift my hand some and she lifts hers. She takes a step back and walks around toward me. When within earshot, she says, simply, "hey."

I return the gesture and smile at the shimmering pool. She stands next to me, but there are four inches of pure, Christian space between us.

"You're lucky, you know," she says.

"What do you mean?"

"You get to travel with a companion."

At first, I don't know what she's talking about and so I ask again, "how do you mean?"

"Your son. You have somebody to spend your evenings

with when you go to sleep. You don't have to do it alone."

"Oh," I say.

"I talk to Jesus all the time. I thank Him for allowing me to be a small part of this important time in the world. But it's nice to be with someone. A body you can feel or hear snoring when it's only the crickets making sounds."

"I suppose so," I say.

She puts a hand between my shoulder blades and it feels nice. Her touch is very soft. Warm. "He's not talking to you, is he?"

"Who?"

"Elliot."

"No," I say.

"He'll come around. I'll be praying for you tonight."

"Thanks."

"If you ever want to talk, you can talk to me you know? Jesus ain't the only person you can unload on."

"Thanks," I say again.

She goes back to her side of the horseshoe and then into her room. I stare at her door for a bit, thinking nice thoughts about her. I turn away from the pool and open the door to my room. Elliot sleeps on top his covers. His snore is mild and subtle. Small and childlike. Innocent. I pull a sheet off my bed and use it to cover Elliot so that I don't wake him.

It's nearly ten o'clock. I don't feel tired. Our mornings usually start early and our evenings usually end early. I lie in my bed and close my eyes. I think about the people I'm with and how our journey will end. I briefly think about what might happen if the rapture never comes. I briefly think about if I'll be found and if my son will be taken away. I have my doubts about some of these things and I weigh my doubts on the probability of these things. I try to stop thinking.

Elliot snores and the room is otherwise quiet.

An hour goes by and I still lie awake. I look at the ceiling. Seems blank and smooth with the lights out. The television, deep and black, infinite in its darkness. It stares at me like a monolithic devil-eye, reading the darkness in me, and for a moment, I am afraid of it. The pastor told us specifically not to turn the televisions on because the liberal media aired stories about us. About our cause and only served as distractions orchestrated by Satan at this crucial time in humanity's history.

I reach over, grab the remote to the television, and press the red button. The TV flickers on and the black eye brightens to blinding. My eyes adjust and I turn to the news. A woman with sandy blond hair talks to me though the glass. She is pleasant and I like her very much. She reminds me of my ex-wife in her sweetness. In her smile. There is a story, though, about domestic missionaries warning the country about the end of the world. The news reporters do a bad job hiding their laughter. Or a bad job pretending to hide laughter. *Nightline* comes on next and I watch it until I fall asleep with the pale light shining through my eyelids. I sleep for about two hours.

The television screeches and buzzes. The sound, harsh and very loud.

I am awake again.

I bat around for the remote and turn the volume down. Elliot continues to sleep, breathing deeply. My eyes adjust to the brightness and I read the red bar with white text scrolling across the screen. An Amber Alert. A picture of a little boy with large brown eyes and brown hair that just barely covers his eyebrows. Elliot's second grade picture. Following it is a picture of me. In the picture, I wasn't smiling and apparently hadn't shaved in several days. I wore one of those button up shirts with flowers printed on them. I looked like a homeless man who'd just robbed one of the Beach Boys. Then, pressure guilt and a stabbing fear all thud in and between my ribs and I begin to perspire. I turn off the television and look over at my son who is still quietly snoring. I reach in my book bag and pull out a bottle of Klonopin my doctor prescribed to me for anxiety. I take two and then a third and, within a few minutes or so, feel okay again.

I look at my son and then to the television, again staring at me. I sit up in the dark, unable to go back to sleep. I put a blanket over the TV and, eventually, the night passes over the two of us.

■ ■ ■

The next morning, when the pastor gets back from Kinko's, we board the church van. All five of us. I direct Elliot into the van as we enter through the sliding door when the pastor places a hand on my shoulder and asks me to speak with him in private. I tell Elliot to get on the van and
that I'll be there in a minute.

"Yes?" I say. I can feel exhaustion like ants under my skin, and I'm certain that it's written all over my face and under my unrested eyelids.

"Michael," he starts. "In the window of your room last night, I could see the light from the television."

"Oh," I say.

"I really want to stress how harmful it can be in this delicate time to be negatively influenced by the media," he says. "I didn't knock on your door because I didn't want to wake Elliot."

"Right," I say. "I'm just having trouble sleeping lately is all. That why it was on."

"I understand, but I don't want anyone watching the media. Liberals and Jews will try to turn us from our end goal. Jesus is coming and they don't want us to believe that."

"I know. I won't do it again."

"Okay," he says. "I won't tell the others, but I'd like your word."

"Okay," I say. "You have my word."

"Alright, then." He says, pats my arm, and we board the van and head for Georgia.

Three weeks until rapture.

. . .

My thoughts stay on the Amber Alert and Elliot. Of the adults, Mary-Ellen keeps my company the most. A few towns back, I faked a foot injury, wrapped my right ankle in an Ace bandage, and started to have her do small favors for me. At one point, we stop for food at a McDonalds and I send her inside to get Elliot's and my food. Surely, I think, if there are mothers who watch the news for missing children, the playground of a McDonald's could be a hotspot. Admittedly, I've used Mary-Ellen's kindness to my advantage, but at the same time, I do enjoy her company. She is smart and smells nice, even when we go a few days without a hotel or a campsite with proper plumbing, there is always the smell of lavender in her skin.

The pastor has picked up a couple of people to join our crusade. One, a red-headed man with crooked teeth who is very personable and loves to talk. He has brought white matching T-shirts for all of us. The shirts have a black cross on the front and the date of the rapture on the back with the words, "It's not too late to find Jesus." He's even brought a shirt that is Elliot's size, which he refuses to wear.

A new lady, I know only as Ms. Lee has joined us as well. She is quite old and her fingers are crooked and gnarled. Of the group, I'm the most reserved. Ms. Lee smiles at me and frequently calls me the quiet one. "Blessed are the meek," they tell me. I take my Kolonpin more frequently now and in secret, worrying when I might run out. These people don't know that my child's face is on the TV because they are not allowed to watch the television. They don't know that I have committed a crime that is, perhaps, unforgivable—from which I cannot backpedal.

Too many people now ride with us. I now think I hate the fat, rich man named Hank because I frequently catch his eyes gazing at Elliot and me just before he turns and looks elsewhere. I can't tell what he wants or is constantly looking at, but I want to remove his eyes in a violent way.

. . .

I hobble out of the van and continue to fake my injury. Mary-Ellen suggests crutches, but I assure her that the injury was only a simple ankle roll and that surely I'd be better in a few days. So I make do with my fake hobbling. My lies have stacked and I am having trouble keeping up with everything I've invented. I wonder if the pastor has told lies himself. Does he believe in the pending Armageddon or is he searching for purpose like the rest of the souls probably are on this trip?

We, as a group—more like a pack—walk to the entrance of a mall somewhere in Georgia. I stopped paying attention to where exactly we were. I originally felt nervous about walking around a mall, much for the same reason I felt weird about walking into a McDonalds, but the mall is a small one, and the town seems obscure, and the people here probably don't read or watch the news. *Hicks*, I think. I hold Elliot's hand as we approach. The large automatic doors to the mall rattle and screech open and we walk inside. The pastor huddles us in a tight circle and talks to us about a plan of action. That we should spread out and be discrete. That security could very well escort us out since we haven't acquired the proper permissions to be here, but that God's message was more important than man's rules. He gives us his speech that I've nearly memorized and before he sets us loose, he looks at me and winks and smiles. Those teeth. White like winter mint.

And so, we split up. Elliot and I, the only ones to stick together. Mary-Ellen goes upstairs and I take to bottom floor. The mall was not very large, but I was still able to lose the others and when I felt no one was looking, I quit faking my limp. I find a bench and Elliot and I sit ourselves down.

I look at the stack of tracts in my hand and I flip through them. It hadn't occurred to me until now, but I haven't actually read any. Inside is a comic strip. The first scene is of three friends driving a car and two of them—including the driver—vanish in a poof of smoke, leaving one passenger in the car to crash into a telephone pole. The man survives the car accident and his friends have been apparently raptured away. The story then follows this survivor after the rapture and shows the aftermath in gruesome and often gory detail. People screaming for their lives. People who are lost and in need of saving. I take the tracts out of Elliot's hands, stack them with mine and throw all of them in the trashcan beside me.

"Why did you do that?" Elliot asks me after having been quiet for several days.

"Because," I say, thinking of a lie. "They were bad prints," is what I finally come up with. I reach in my pocket and pull out a small white pill, pop it in my mouth and swallow it dry. A vicodin. Jeffery gave me a couple for my foot injury. We both agreed to keep our arrangement from the rest of the group.

"You want some ice cream?" I ask my son and he nods affirmatively. I take his hand and we walk to a Chick-Fil-A in one of the corners of the mall. I found it strange that this mall didn't have a food court, just random fast food restaurants built in random corners. With the twenty dollars the pastor allotted me, I purchase Elliot a small vanilla milkshake with no cherry. We walk around the mall aimlessly for a bit, and I promise Elliot that we'll look in a toy store later and maybe I'll get him something. He smiles at this idea, and for a moment I think that he loves me again. I briefly squeeze his hand tighter but lovingly and relax my grip.

We meander upstairs to the second floor. Admittedly, I do this in hopes of running in to Mary-Ellen but mainly because I know a toy store is somewhere along the way. As we walk, I look down to the bottom floor, where we just were, and watch the various patrons. Mothers strolling around their babies. Old people with bright pink or green visors, doing laps. All folks, carrying on about their lives as though the world is not ending. As though life will be okay and that they are safe in their bubbles, in their mall, in whatever lies they've told themselves to stay as happy as they seem. I see the pastor by a fake fichus tree planted in fake brown dirt, passing out tracts he made at Kinko's. I can read his rapture shirt clearly from several yards away. He stands not far from the trash can where I dumped my tracts and when he asks me later, I will tell him that I passed all of them out. Then, he will tell me how proud God is of me.

I look back up at a paternity store across the way and see no one inside besides a large man dressed in a blue muumuu and a large floppy hat. The man disappears behind some clothing racks, so I take Elliot's hand and walk around to get a better look. I only want to walk by, to satisfy a curiosity. When closer, I can see his bare feet and hairy legs stand from under the large flowered dress. Dimpled arms adjust the floppy hat as the man looks himself in a mirror. Elliot and I take a bench near the entrance of the store and I position myself so that I can only see this man's head over the racks and shelves. He takes the floppy hat off, revealing a balding head with hair only on the sides—a deep horseshoe of baldness. For an instant, I think it is Hank dressing like a woman, but I couldn't be sure. Too far inside the store and behind the clothes. I turn my head and decide not to look any more. Decide that I don't want to know for sure.

A week from today, the world will come to an end. And I am waiting.

・・・

Nylon tents stand like half-bubbles surrounding the gentle breathings of orange fire. The campsite is dark and pinholes of stars light the sky like, as the pastor says, heaven waiting for us on the other side. The pastor feeds the fire and is the only one to do so. The twelve of us sit around the fire, feeling the heat, the pressure of it. Mary-Ellen sits to my left, Elliot to my right. The pastor is speaking on Hebrews 10:24-25, about the importance of sticking together and worshiping God as an assembly as "The Day" approaches. Now, less than a week away.

Elliot holds a Clif Bar in his hands and his hands rest in his lap. He chews a bit of the small bland meal. He swallows what is in his mouth and he turns to me, and in a low voice that I don't think anyone else can hear, he asks what the difference between Jewish people and Christian people is. I explain to him that the Jews don't believe in Jesus and we do. He asks me what is going to happen to his mother when Jesus comes back. I tell him that's up to Jesus, though I feel that this could be a lie, that non-believers don't have a pass. He asks me what will happen to him since he is part Jewish. I tell him that he will be fine.

He is quiet for a while and after a minute or two, he leans in close to my ear and whispers, "I don't think I believe in Jesus." I see Hank glance our way, but his eyes flicker straight ahead at the pastor. I tell him not to say that and, when I do, I can see a switch in his brain turn off again. He chews back on his bar and stares, mesmerized at the fire, not responding to my whispers. Mary-Ellen slips her fingers between mine and grips tightly, smiling at me and glancing at my boy.

In the light of the fire, Elliot looks to be drifting and I send him to bed. He goes, unzips the nylon door, and disappears inside our pathetic residence. After the fire begins to die off, the others move to their own tents and disband, and I return to my tent with my son. He has fallen asleep with a headlamp on and a comic book about zombies lying open across his chest that I did not buy for him. I don't think he reads the words and that he only flips through the grotesque pictures of people eating people. I pick up the comic and hide it under my pillow. I'll toss it tomorrow. I carefully turn off his light and curl under my sleeping bag. I fall asleep to his snoring.

■ ■ ■

Last night, we had dinner at the Olive Garden and thanked the Lord for providing these past several weeks. Elliot had again turned mute but he ate his food politely and bowed his head when everyone else bowed their heads. I would look at Elliot while the pastor prayed for a swift rapture, and all the while I hoped that the next day would pass like any other.

Today, the dates on our T-shirts finally match the dates on our receipts and calendars and cell phones. The day is a cloudy one. Appropriate enough for the end of the world, I suppose. I'm sure everyone else thinks the same but doesn't speak on the matter. The pastor says he's saved up just enough money to get a final hotel room, which he's paid for with his debit card. Only one room and we all sit in a circle inside the room. The pastor instructs us to flip the twin beds horizontally like cockroaches on their sides and against the wall so that we'd have more space. The pastor told us that the time of the rapture is only an estimation and that it could be an hour or more after the prediction, but that our time has undoubtedly come and to await God to grasp and lift our souls and hearts out of this world, soon to be expired.

We extend and interlock our fingers with one another. Elliot sits between Mary-Ellen and me. I, begrudgingly, hold Hank's hand to my right. Jeffery, the black man with the lazy eye, Ms. Lee, the older lady with gnarled fingers, and others complete the circle. The pastor instructs us to close our eyes and everyone does. I look at my shoes, though. I want to make sure Elliot is doing the same and—from what I can tell—he is. The pastor leads us in a prayer, speaking to God and thanking him for all His blessings and His grace. He continues to pray for what seems like a half an hour, nonstop. My legs get uncomfortable and I can hear the shifting of the others as their legs become the same kind of restless.

The pastor stops praying.

He doesn't say "amen," he simply stops talking. I assume this means the time is coming and still it doesn't. People sniff and cough and become more uncomfortable. Elliot squirms and at one point lies on his side, putting his head in Mary-Ellen's lap. I don't let go of his hand. He breathes heavily through his nose and relaxes his grip. I still have his tiny fingers. Hank's meaty hand is now wet and slimy. I don't like it. I close my eyes all the way to clear my mind. It does little to help.

I hear screaming outside of the hotel door, far away screams. Small gasps and whimpers from our group react to the sounds. "The time has come, brothers and sisters," the pastor reassures us. Hank tightens his grip and I feel my bones collapse together like one of those Chinese fans. He is afraid. I am afraid. A loud thud. A bang. Someone wants in.

"Take us, Jesus!" I hear someone in our room announce. Elliot sits up at this and tightens his grip on my hand and I am appreciative of it. A grown man and a small child clinging to me, both, much in the same way. The bang becomes louder and deafening, like someone trying to punch a hole through the air and through our heads, but I keep my eyes closed. The shattering of wood and splinters. The explosion of force and stomping. People from my group scream. Elliot is screaming. It occurs to me that Jesus simply doesn't want me. But my eyes stay closed and I tell Elliot to keep his closed as well. What feels like a dozen arms wrap underneath mine and they are not gentle. The arms tug at me and my body floats off the ground before I fall on my back. My hands still grip Elliot's and Hank's. A force lands on my side and I think it has broken one or several of my ribs. I yelp in pain. The arms and the voices—dark and unintelligible—pull harder and Hank's sweaty hand slips from mine.

"Jesus, help us!" I hear. The noises sound like hell. Like suffering and pain. My eyes are still closed and I continue to believe. One set of hands is on my freed right arm and another set of hands on my left—the one gripping Elliot's. The force rips us apart. I lose him and his tiny fingers. I can still feel his sweat in the palm of my hand as I am thrown on my stomach and my cheekbone lands on the hard, carpeted floor. I hear Elliot being lifted far away and his cries fade into the distance. All the while, I keep my eyes closed. Because I don't want to see. I don't want to see the truth of the matter. I only hear the screams. The chaos. The constant abrogating nature of my relationships. My relationship with my wife and son. With God, even. But with my eyes closed I will tell myself lies and Elliot will tell himself lies, as will the others, because for now, the lies will do. Lies that life will get better, that the seven adults on this journey will eventually ascend to something grander. Happier. Yes, for the time being, I suppose the lies will do.

Super Tuscan
Justin Campbell

"Can I start you off with some drinks this evening? Wine perhaps? One of our delightful cocktails?" The waiter stood with his hands behind his back, as they settled themselves into their chairs. He had a pencil thin mustache. The woman looked down at the menu. Her husband looked up at the waiter.

"Water sounds good."

"Sparkling or still?"

The man looked across the table at his parents. His mother raised her eyebrows as she scanned the wine list. "I prefer sparkling."

Her husband smiled. "Sparkling it is."

Her in-laws had been trying to set this dinner up for weeks. She scanned the menu, as the waiter, dressed in all white, walked away to get their water. The woman did not speak or read Italian and glanced over at her husband to see if he understood what he was reading. His brow was furrowed in concentration as he stared at the tiny print. He looked over at his parents. "How about an appetizer?"

Her father-in-law nodded. "Calamari?"

The woman squirmed in her chair and tapped her husband's foot under the table. He glanced over at her, before responding. "How about Bruchetta?"

His father peered over the top of his menu. "Since when do you not like calamari?"

The man smiled. "I love calamari."

"Calamari it is, then." His father waved down the waiter.

"Yes, sir. Are you ready to order?"

"Two orders of calamari, please."

"Anything else?"

"Yes. A bottle of Antionori 'Solaia'. The 2006."

"Of course, sir. Anything else?"

"That's it for now."

The woman pulled a piece of bread from the basket and began to butter it. Her mother-in-law leaned over and began to speak in a low voice. "You remember my friend Josie? The one who got you your china set?" The woman nodded. Her mother-in-law continued. "She just discovered she had a gluten allergy." The older woman glanced down at the bread. "It's actually a kind of blessing, if you ask me."

The man rolled his eyes. "Mom."

His mother shrugged her shoulders. "I'm only remarking on the negative impact gluten has on the American physique. It goes straight to our hips, our thighs, our buttocks."

The woman took a small bite of bread and chewed it until it was the consistency of lukewarm oatmeal.

"What's the update from the station?"

The man looked at his father. "I thought we agreed not to not to talk about this."

"A man can't ask his son about his work?"

"I don't work there yet."

"They need to hire you. God knows we need better firefighters in this city."

The man set his menu down. "I'm working on it."

The woman took a sip of her sparkling water. She hated the blandness of it. The carbon dioxide slid down the back of her throat. It tickled. "He got a bad review last week."

Everyone at the table looked at her. She broke off another small piece of bread and chewed on it. The waiter walked up before anyone had a chance to respond. He was holding a dark bottle with an orange foil and a tan label. When he reached their table, he presented the bottle to her father-in-law. "The 2006 Antinori 'Solaia'."

Her father-in-law stared at her husband. "You got a bad

review? For what?"

The waiter was still standing there, holding the wine at an angle. "Would you like me too—"

"Pour the damn wine, already!"

The waiter nodded and began to pour. The man shook his head. "It's not a big deal."

His mother shook her head. "One usually doesn't receive bad reviews for nothing."

The man picked up his menu. "Do we all know what we're getting?"

The waiter had finished pouring and had walked away. His father took a sip of the wine. "We're not through talking about this."

The man glanced at his wife. She avoided his gaze by trying to figure out what ingredients were in each dish. The restaurant was a new favorite of her in-laws. She turned the menu over, curious to see how much the wine they were drinking was. It was listed as a "Super Tuscan" and it was very, very expensive.

. . .

"Do you know what you'd like to order?"

"I think so." The man looked up. "You ready, mom?" His mother nodded. The waiter turned to her, notepad in hand.

"For you, ma'am?"

"I'll take the asparagus and poached egg. From the small plates menu."

"Anything else?"

"Can I have a box with my meal?"

"Of course, ma'am." The waiter turned to the woman.

"For you?"

The woman looked up from the menu she had begun to read again. "Could you come back to me?"

"Of course." He turned toward her father-in-law. "For you sir?"

His father looked at the waiter over the top of his reading glasses. "I'll take the *ossobucco alla Milanese*."

"Of course, sir." The waiter turned toward the man. "For you?"

The man pointed at his father. "I'll have what he's having."

"Very good." The waiter scribbled down the order and turned to the woman. "Are you ready?"

The woman chewed on her lower lip. "I think I'll have the *capellini*."

Her mother-in-law leaned over. "You should get a box with that."

The man rolled his eyes. "Let her order, mom."

His mother shrugged. "I'm only trying to help."

The woman handed her menu to the waiter.

. . .

She had eaten all of it. As she ate, she tried to eat it slowly. She tried to savor the tomatoes, the garlic, the thyme. The entire meal, she ate knowing that her mother-in-law was watching her every bite. The older woman was nibbling on a stalk of asparagus, having already placed half of her small meal in the box as soon as she received her plate. The woman, on the other hand, couldn't keep from shoveling the food from her plate into her mouth. There were moments, when she thought she had eaten enough. Then, she'd look down and keep eating. Soon, her plate was clean. They were sitting there, waiting for the plates to be cleared. Her mother-in-law dabbed at the corners of her mouth with her napkin, careful not to smudge her lipstick. She looked over at the woman. "You eating for two tonight?"

The woman felt sweat begin to form under her arms. She looked over at her husband. He cleared his throat and took a sip of water. The woman pushed her plate away from her. Her mother-in-law looked around the table. "It was a joke, people."

The woman looked down at the white table cloth. It was speckled with red dots and covered in bread crumbs. "I don't like what you're implying."

"It was a joke, dear."

The man shifted in his chair. "Mom—"

"Don't you lecture me."

The man hung his head. "Would you just let me—"

His mother shook her head. "I can't believe this. I knew this would happen. I told your father as we were driving in. We can't even have a family meal together without someone getting their feelings hurt." Her eyes started to well up with tears. "I am sick and tired of being mistreated by my own flesh and blood. Do you know how long I was in labor with you?"

The man sighed. "Yes, mother."

"*Twenty-seven hours!* That's more than a day!" She wiped her eyes with the back of her hand. "Is this is what I get in return?"

His father patted her hand. "It's ok."

The woman glanced over at her husband. He shrugged his shoulders. The woman leaned back in her chair. "We're pregnant."

Her mother-in-law's eyes widened through her tears. "Excuse me?"

"We're pregnant."

His mother began to smile. "Why didn't you tell us?"

"You didn't give us a chance."

"How far along are you?"

"Thirteen weeks. As of yesterday."

"Well," his mother said, crying even more now, "I had no idea you were."

The man reached over and grabbed his wife's hand out of her lap. "It's ok, mom. Water under the bridge."

The woman glanced over at her husband and pulled her hand away. Her mother-in-law dried her eyes with her napkin. "We'll have to have the shower at the Regent's Library downtown. We can use the room that faces the garden. I have this girl, you'll love her, she'd be perfect to do the invitations, and we'll have the same bakery that did your wedding cake, though now that I think about it, cupcakes would probably be more fitting—"

The waiter had walked up to the table. "Will you be having dessert tonight?"

The man shook his head. His father raised his hands in a sign of defeat. His mother smiled and shook her head. The woman, glancing down at the menu at the center of the table, looked back up at the waiter.

"I would like the chocolate soufflé."

"That will take at least twenty minutes, ma'am."

"I can wait."

"Of course, ma'am."

"I'll take a coffee too. Decaf."

"Very good."

The woman sat back as the waiter walked away. She looked at the older woman sitting across the table from her.

"You were saying?"

The Death of an Unblinded Man
April Rosemary Ehrlich

An elaborate series of textbooks, novels, essays, poems, and plays had to be read to the blind Elliot William Kasminski before he could attain a degree in English, making him the only student of his class who had never seen what a single word looked like. Of course, he could feel letters when corporeal in form, and thus had an idea of how they might appear, such the letter P, which was like a ladle balancing on its handle, then if it were to fall over it would become a little b. The letter O is an onion ring, and if you were to take a bite out of it, it would become a C. Meanwhile, the letter A looks like two fallen people who are using their arms to push each other back into place, and H is A before the two people fell, or after they pushed themselves back into place—he decided that it was consistently both, so in the world of letters, H becomes A becomes H becomes A, so the two people together create laughter—HAHAHAHA. But his favorite is S, which Elliot visualized as an earthworm crawling back and forth wondering, *Where am I going?* And so, that exact question threaded through his existing thoughts when he felt the letter S, such as in the sign, NO SMOKING...*Where am I going?* SALE! SALE! SALE!...*Where am I going?* SEATTLE, WA...*Where am I going?*

Elliott was not born blind, but small. At one o'clock post meridiem, on June 21, 1976, Elliott William Kasminski entered the world as a five-and-a-half-pound infant during the blindingly dry midst of summer, which weeks later would have offered this to the infant's developing eyes: dust particles dancing in pale beams of light, clear waves rising from hot asphalt, sprinkler water clinging to a rusty window screen. All of these moments will happen, did happen, after Elliot's moment of birth, but as the infant screamed and stretched his rat-skinned fingers to catch something of this future world, he was rushed into an incubator where an oversupply of oxygen permanently destroyed an optic nerve necessary for vision.

And so, the blind infant grew into a blind boy who developed into a blind man who graduated with a degree in English, all the while he grasped too tightly onto this idea of nearly seeing aerial dust, heat waves rising from asphalt, sprinkler droplets. Unsurprisingly, Elliott became addicted to visual beauty, or at least the closest of which he could obtain through descriptive imageries provided by literature. To him, the mystic grandeur of lions would have never existed without Ernest Hemingway, while the affinity between ocean and sky was designed by James Joyce, and Leo Tolstoy was responsible for the way a woman's cheeks blushed when bitten by snow. Of course, Elliott realized that his mind's interpretations of such images could never be entirely accurate; and yet, what was accuracy? Elliot often remembered some lines that clung to his mind post-graduation: *Every mind composes its own visual perception based off environmental influences such as education, where we learn to conform to concepts such as the color red, the color blue, which only allow society to successfully run as a communicative whole, but in reality there is no way of knowing how each individual visually perceives things. What is really red? What is really blue? Each human being may physically see such things differently than all the others. Thus, we are all blind.* These lines were slight reassurances that kept Elliott alive and well until the day he was unblinded.

At three-thirty post meridiem, on July 18, 1999, an overly tanned woman named Franny was dusting a bathroom rug out the window of her fifth story Los Angeles apartment, singing, *Here comes the sun, here comes the sun, and I say it's all right!* just before her bronzed right elbow knocked over a Carnegiea gigantea cactus, potted in an Aztec-style orange bowl, sending it tumbling past the window of the fourth story apartment where an old man was feeding his cat, Raleigh, and singing *mew mew mew*, then past the window of the third story apartment where a well-dressed mother was telling her straight-backed daughter, *A French braid will win over any man's heart*, then twirling past the second story apartment where a toddler named Vincent was witnessing a potted cactus shatter atop the head of Elliott William Kaminksi, a blind twenty-three-year-old graduate who had been waiting for the three-thirty-five bus to arrive.

Sun, sun, sun, here it comes.

A firework burst in the center of Elliott's skull. He winced and cried and moaned and opened his eyes to attain his life's second vision: two glassy blue eyes staring directly into his.

Are you OK?

She was a girl of maybe twelve. Pieces of her blond hair fell off her shoulders and glowed white from the sun standing behind her. Elliott's eyes shrieked from the pain of her excruciating luminosity, whereas his chest heaved and lost breath due to her stunning brilliance. She was an overload of light and beauty, and so Elliott's heart skipped a beat.

His eyes darted and caught onto other imageries: a woman, lanky as a crane, pulling her daughter by the elbow; a cacti living its last moments amid shattered pottery; a moonfaced boy staring from a second story window, watching, just as the moon might—with wisdom and cold security. *I know you*, the boy seemed to say. *I know you, and I know that you were once born, and I know that you will soon die.* Every beautiful sight sent Elliot's chest leaping for breath, which established his life-threatening disposition: to Elliott, everything was beautiful. He inhaled sharply as his heart fluttered once, twice, then three times before he draped a sweating palm over his eyes.

And now, the peril: Elliot stood so close to the edge of something that his toes curled over its jagged ridge; a wavering body deciding whether to fall backward or fall forward. Unveiling his eyes would allow Elliot to see all that he has tried to imagine—he would know what is red, what is blue—and yet, he risked the possibility of his suddenly weak heart bursting from the infinite revelations of sight.

Or, he could simply keep his eyes closed. Elliot could keep a bandana tied firmly around his skull, like a child swinging at a piñata while everyone else jeers and screams. Everyone could see the dancing animal and they could see him, clumsily falling about, swinging and missing, swinging and missing. They could laugh and they could jeer and scream. They could see!

At three-forty-four post meridiem, on July 18, 1999, Elliot William Kasminski removed a tremulous palm from his eyes, and he saw everything. *There is beauty in this world!* His heart fluttered and shook, pained, and burst, and he died a happy, unblinded man.

The Best We Can
William Cass

My parents told me about my mother's affair, if it could be called that, when we met at the St. Francis Hotel in San Francisco just after I'd turned thirty. They'd come out from Pittsburgh and were staying there for one of my father's last business conventions before his retirement. I'd flown down from a teaching job in Juneau, Alaska to see them and stay with an old friend from college.

Their room was on the thirty-fourth floor. They sat side by side in tall, elegant armchairs separated by a small table. I leaned against the headboard of their bed stretched out across from them. It was about 4:30 in the afternoon, and through the big windows behind my parents, the late October light had already begun to fall over the city.

When I'd first arrived, my father had made us all vodka tonics. We'd caught up on my brothers and sister, how my father's keynote speech had gone the night before, and the progress on the retirement home they were building in Hilton Head, South Carolina. Then he simply said, "Your mother has a bit of news. She's slept with her old boyfriend from high school."

The room was still for a long moment until my mother said evenly, "'Slept' is an exaggeration. We were in the backseat of his car at a park. It was over like that."

She clicked her fingers. They both looked at me blankly.

I shook my head slowly. "I don't know what to say. I can't believe it."

"Neither could I," my father said. He took a long swallow from his drink and held the glass on the top of his knee.

My mother sighed. "It was just a ridiculous, impulsive thing. One time. Never before. Never again. I was in an emotional state. It was when I was up there in Connecticut to move your grandpa into the convalescent hospital."

I sat forward and blurted, "The back of his car?"

"He'd heard I was there to move Daddy's things. It's a small town. He came by the house one night. We went for a drive."

She shrugged. They both continued to look at me intently. It seemed like they were waiting for me to pass some sort of judgment.

Finally, I asked, "Do the other kids know?"

My father shook his head. "You're the oldest."

I extended my gaze over their heads at the dwindling light against the tops of the city's buildings and wondered why my mother had told him anything about it at all.

I looked back and forth at each of them and asked, "So what happens now?"

My father pursed his lips. "I don't know. We don't know. No current plans. The truth is…" He shook the ice in his glass. "The truth is I've ignored your mother for some time… her needs."

I'm not sure what it was I saw on my father's face at that moment, whether it was fear or vulnerability or something else, but I knew I'd never seen it there before. The rock solid stoicism I'd grown to simply accept as his persona—the star athlete, the successful corporate executive, the stern family patriarch—was gone.

"We haven't been emotionally available to each other for some time," my mother said.

"Whatever it's called," my father mumbled.

I watched my mother lower her face, then turn it away from him toward the hotel room door.

I ended the awkwardness shortly after that by contriving excuses to leave. We made vague arrangements to have brunch together the next morning before they flew home.

But before the elevator had even reached the lobby, I knew I would break those plans. I had nothing more to ask or say to them about what they'd told me and couldn't imagine making small talk about anything else.

I relocated to Seattle a couple of summers later and met the woman who would become my wife at an orientation for teachers new to the district where we were both hired. After the wedding, we were able to buy a small, older home just up from Lake Washington on the Eastside, and worked together fixing it up for the next few years until our son, Ben, was born. No one could have prepared us for that. He was severely disabled with a smorgasbord of developmental, physical, and neurological problems. He spent the first six weeks after birth in the NIC-U where the dysmorphologist who treated him there told us that kids like Ben rarely survived more than a handful of years. He was in and out of the hospital thereafter every few months for pneumonias and surgeries. It was during one of those admittances when Ben was seven that my wife announced that she'd become involved with another teacher at her school. She said they were moving together to Madison, Wisconsin, to enroll in a graduate program in art history, a subject in which I'd never known her to have any interest.

At the time, we were sitting in a little anteroom in the med-surg wing at Seattle Children's Hospital waiting for Ben's surgeon to come let us know how the procedure to insert a feeding tube into his stomach had gone.

She said, "I'm done being a martyr. I need to take care of myself. I have a right to be happy."

"But," I stammered, "you never said a word. I didn't know…never had the chance…"

She looked at me coldly. Her eyes narrowed. "I can't worry about your feelings. I can only deal with my own."

The surgeon entered the room, still wearing his scrubs and

operating cap. He smiled and said, "Everything went well. Everything is going to be all right."

She nodded earnestly in that way she did when listening to someone. It had the effect of making the speaker feel immediately connected, acknowledged, and respected. So, the surgeon directed the rest of his comments to her. I sat numb and didn't hear a word he said.

After my wife left, Ben had to stay in the medically fragile center of the hospital for better than a year because the first fundoplication had gone bad right away and the doctors decided upon a very gradual and careful titration of his feeds with the new feeding tube. He stayed on a continuous twenty-hour drip for seven weeks before they were finally able to slowly increase his intervals to greater bolus volumes. Towards the end of that time, he had a tracheotomy to help manage his secretions and then two additional surgeries to move his testicles down their canals closer to where they would have normally been. The customary recovery time was involved after each, so it was several more months before I could begin trying to arrange the contract home nursing needed to have him discharged. In the end, I was able to find nursing to cover my work hours, but overnight shifts only three times a week, so had to manage the rest myself. His care needs were round-the-clock, so I didn't have a lot of time for much else.

My parents made a yearly visit to Seattle for a week each spring. Over the ensuing years after that afternoon in San Francisco, nothing ever changed in their relationship that I could see. It seemed to me that they had fashioned their mutual co-existence with something between bewildered acceptance and silent resignation. In retirement, my father's countenance and self-reliance gradually deflated like a balloon left behind a couch, and this became exacerbated as his hearing loss worsened, even with the most technologically advanced of aids. His golf games dwindled from four or five a week to once or twice a month, a decline that accompanied the degree to which my parents associated with friends. More and more, their days involved long periods of time sitting in separate blue recliners in front of the television reading sections of the newspaper, while my father kept one eye on whatever sports show played and my mother shouted tidbits to him from articles that caught her fancy over the volume's din.

Their collective general health slowly deteriorated. After my father's second heart attack and my mother's first, we convinced them to move closer to one of the kids. They finally sold their place and bought a cottage in a lovely graduated assisted living community on the Deschutes River in Bend, Oregon, near my sister, Beth, and her family. That made sense because she was the youngest and still had two small children with whom my parents planned to help. Although that assistance never materialized, Beth or her husband could take them to their medical appointments and lend a hand in managing their other affairs as needed, so it was an improved arrangement. However, shortly after arriving, my father began waxing nostalgic for Hilton Head, claimed that we forced him to move, and bitterness began to invade the shell that quickly became his final internal retreat.

On their last visit before my father died, my mother brought some old photographs to give me. She said she'd chosen a batch for each of the kids because they'd otherwise just sit untouched in a box in their attic. I looked through them that first morning as we ate breakfast together at my dining room table. It was already warm, so I had the French doors to the porch open. Ben sat in his wheelchair in the doorway where he could feel the sunlight across his lap and squawk when he heard the birds.

The order and arrangement of the photos seemed to be completely random. There were some of my parents as far back as their days together at the University of Connecticut and then snippets of various family members—mostly different combinations of my four siblings and me, and later of our own families—over the years at holidays, vacations, and special occasions. Because they were so scattered, I found myself arranging them chronologically and, in so doing, watching us all grow and age in rapid succession.

I laid two photographs of my parents that struck me side by side on the table. They were both engrossed in their newspapers and didn't even glance over. One snapshot was black and white from their honeymoon. My father had his arm around my mother, squinting with one eye into the sun behind the camera. They were leaning against a railing in front of a waterfall: handsome, robust, their serene expressions full of confidence and promise.

The second couldn't have been taken too long before that first photo. In it, they sat side by side at the little wicker table on their screened-in back porch in Hilton Head picking crab from shells in a bowl. It must have been among their last crabbing outings there, which was one of their only shared pastimes. They'd walk down under the bridge below the lagoon behind their house, and my mother would toss a chicken neck tied to a six-foot string out into the brackish shallows at low tide. When a blue shell crab approached and began to follow the bait, she would slowly recoil the string towards the bank where my father waited with a long-handled net to try to snatch it up and drop it in a plastic bucket. On a good day, they could coax seven or eight crabs into the bucket in a couple of hours. I knew that it reminded them fondly, as it did me, of our crabbing and clamming excursions years before on the Connecticut shore or at Cape Cod. In the picture, my father wore a startled expression and my mother grinned with her fingertips on his knee.

Somewhere in between those two photographs, they'd raised a family, our family. My mother always chuckled over the chaos of the period of time when were all growing up; she said that those years were just a blur.

Two things happened when Ben turned twelve that were significant. The first occurred on a rainy Sunday afternoon in the late fall. I took him to the IMAX theater at the planetarium to see a new movie that had opened about the Annapurna Sanctuary in Nepal where I'd trekked when I was younger. The theater had a small disabled seating section off to the side for wheelchairs with a couple of folding chairs for companions. A woman about my age already occupied one of the chairs. She was pretty. In the wheelchair next to her, a man was tilted back ready for viewing. His tongue lolled out of the side of the mouth. She wiped the drool off his chin with a blue paisley bandana that was tucked into the collar of his shirt.

I arranged Ben in a similar fashion and sat down in the chair next to her. When I glanced over, she was smiling gently at me.

"I'm Alice," she said. "This is my husband, Paul."

I shook her hand, introduced Ben and myself, and we talked a bit before the show started. She asked me about Ben's prognosis.

I said, "Undiagnosed genetic syndrome."

"From birth then?"

I nodded. "Paul?"

She sighed. "Car accident a year and a half ago. We were coming home from our daughter's high school graduation."

I swallowed and watched her look at him, then take his hand in his lap.

After the movie, she asked if I'd like to get coffee, and that started us doing things together with Ben and Paul every couple of months. It was nice to spend time with a person with whom I shared similar circumstances. Of course, that was as far as it could go.

The second thing was that, for the first time in his life, Ben hugged me back. It may well have been just an unintentional reflex of some kind because it had never happened before and hasn't since. But that doesn't matter...for a handful of seconds, it did.

Ben's mom asked to see him again not too long ago, eleven years after she left. As far as I know, she never married her lover, but they'd stayed together, and she called when they were passing through the area. They drove over, but he stayed in the car, parked down the street. I don't know how to describe the way I felt when I answered the door—a tumult of emotions, I guess, followed by emptiness. Much as they had with me, the years had taken their toll on her. She held herself with a cordial and dignified removal, but I saw something in her eyes that told me she was still the girl I'd married.

I brought her into Ben's room where he was propped up in his bed in the middle of a feed.

"Benny-boy," she whispered and kissed his forehead. He looked past her at whatever it was that he always gazed at. She rearranged and propped the pillows around him, and I felt the old, painful, instinctive twinge of never doing things well enough for her.

She didn't ask, but I gave her a summary of how Ben had been doing while we both looked at him and she stroked his hair. Then we were silent. I wondered what more it was that we could really talk about. The motor on his feeding pump made its whee-whir.

"I'll give you some time with him," I said and left the room.

I busied myself in the kitchen, unloaded the dishwasher, rinsed out the coffee carafe, threw out the grounds. Then I went into the sunroom, sat on the couch, and tried to grade some papers. At one point, I thought I heard her reading aloud to him from one of the picture books on his shelves. It may have been a book she bought for him; it probably was. After a while, I was sure that I heard her singing softly to him a lullaby that had been a regular one for them when he was an infant.

I looked out the window at the picket fence we'd built together just after we bought the house and before Ben was born. The climbing roses we'd planted on either side of the gate had grown over the arbor into a tangle of red bursts and green foliage that nodded now in the small breeze and sunlight.

It wasn't long before she came to the front door, gave me one of her familiar, sad smiles, and said, "Thank you."

I watched her go down the steps, through the gate, and up the sidewalk to where the car was parked under a tree. I could just make out his figure behind the wheel in the shadows. Ben's pump began to beep, signifying that his feed cycle had finished, and I went to turn it off.

Not long thereafter, my mother was diagnosed with early onset Alzheimer's disease. She was about to turn eighty and had become increasingly forgetful the past few years, so we weren't surprised. Neither was she, though she was frightened by how debilitating the disease had become at the end of her own father's life. Her neurologist put her on a medication that he said might slow the process and directed her to be as active mentally, socially, and physically as possible. She'd moved into an apartment in the lodge after my father's death and already had a fair amount of acquaintances there. With the diagnosis, she increased her canasta games to twice a week and began to take more meals in the dining hall with other residents. She also joined an exercise class and got a subscription to a monthly puzzle magazine. So, she did all right.

She still came here for her most recent visit. Only a short, direct flight was involved, so there weren't any travel problems. But during our last phone conversation, my sister had expressed some new concerns about the dangers of her being on her own much longer. Beth said that not too long before, she'd found a stove burner left on overnight when she went over to the apartment. There was another recent occasion when they'd had to take her to the ER when she'd fainted after confusing some of the medications she'd taken. We both wanted her to maintain as much dignity and independence as possible, but Beth was wondering if the time wasn't approaching when she'd need to move upstairs into skilled nursing, especially in light of the pending transfer to another state that was likely with her husband's work. Beth asked if I could talk to her about it; I said I would.

After we got home from the airport and settled, she did appear to me a little more fitful, more methodical. Maintaining her daily routines seemed especially critical to her: counting out her pills in the morning, taking care of her ileoscopy bag and all that entailed, fixing her tea and crustless toast for breakfast, pouring endlessly over the newspaper, watching her afternoon talk shows on television. She shuffled everywhere, and complained more about how she was always cold, how she couldn't keep any weight on, about the veins in her legs, and her sleeping troubles. The glass rarely seemed half-full.

That first day, we walked up the street with Ben to a little café she'd always liked for lunch. After our meals arrived, she told the waitress that her soup wasn't hot enough and sent it back to be reheated. She commented that the potato salad was all right, but not as flavorful as her own.

I finally said, "Tell me something good, Mom. Something good that's going on with you."

"Well," she said. She took off her glasses and pinched the bridge or her nose before replacing them. I could see that she was trying not to smile. "Warren Marshall has been calling."

"What's that?" I vaguely remembered the name, but couldn't place it.

"Warren. My high school boyfriend."

I thought of that afternoon in the St. Francis Hotel. I said, "How? When?"

"Well, he called after he heard your father had died. And he's called several times since. Just to check on me, he says. We don't talk about much. I don't think his marriage is a very happy one. I'm not sure if he's even married anymore."

She took a sip of soup, it seemed to me, to hide the sparkle in her eyes. The spoon trembled a bit in her hand. I sat back and shook my head. Who knew how many years she had left? I thought about how much of life hinged on those things we could control and those things we couldn't. I thought about how we all just do the best we can.

I heard myself say, "Why don't you find out?"

She shrugged. She looked out the window and set her spoon down. "The last time he called, he talked about taking a trip out this way. He has a grandson who goes to college in Portland. Said he might rent a car and drive down to Bend."

When she looked back at me, her lips were trembling a little, too, her eyes full of hope and fear and uncertainty. She looked so small and frail. In that moment, I knew there was no need for the conversation about skilled nursing; when the time came for that, I'd move her up to live with me. I reached over and put my hand on top of hers. I smiled, and she made a thin attempt to do the same.

After a while, she looked over my shoulder and said, "This is a nice place. It doesn't look new. We should have come here before."

I squeezed her hand and said, "You're right. We should have."

Rheumatic Minutes With My Father
Patrick Falconi

It was a horrible summer. Before the month of August settled in, a dense gauze of blighting heat and intolerable humidity had choked life inside the city. Lobbyists, attorneys and hookers—everyone who ambled the streets of Washington DC—panted through swollen purple lips attached to bloated anemic faces. I walked down Twelfth Street, rounded the corner onto T Street, found a shaded alley between Victorian-style row houses, and took cover from the afternoon heat. I sat down on a patch of grass, leaned my back against the warm bricks that baked throughout the hot morning, and opened my first beer; it was warm and tasted flat. A white pigeon landed on the ground beside my feet, found the dry aluminum drainpipe that hung off the opposite wall, and squeezed inside.

It was a quarter-to-five. Melanie's gallery on U Street closed in forty-five minutes and she would probably be home with the artist just before six o'clock. I leaned forward, peered across the street and gazed at her apartment. Her Persian cat, Fenny, jumped up behind the window, pawed at imaginary insects, was distracted by a passing sparrow and jumped back down. I felt thick, sour foam rise to the bottom of my throat; I gagged, took several long pulls of beer to crush my anxiety, and worried I might vomit. For the past two days I'd been sleeping on brown pine needles under a picnic bench at Gazebo Park in Alexandria. Melanie kicked me out of the apartment, started dating Max, a successful installation artist whose work she began exhibiting less than a week ago, and gently suggested I move back in with my father.

Long black shadows began staining the gray sidewalk like dense patches of clotted ink. A few moments later, narrow lengths of shade stretched over Melanie's apartment like cold iron bars of betrayal. I noticed the warm orange sun tilt lower in the horizon; its bright light reflected against the dark windows and produced a beautiful, but inappropriate color, and somehow reminded me of a faithful woman.

I needed a shower and a change of clothes but dreaded having another argument. Melanie's new boyfriend—whose ingratiating smile had been both derisive and sympathetic—intervened on my behalf by slipping a few greenbacks into my shirt pocket the night before last. I reluctantly accepted his money, got drunk for two consecutive days, and decided to promptly repay the artist by shattering beer bottles against his head at sundown. But as the heat dragged on, my vengeance wavered and gave way to more practical considerations. I swallowed my last sip of warm beer, bid farewell to the pigeon that managed to change directions in the narrow drainpipe, and headed back into Virginia. On my way to the bus stop I decided to pick up some old clothes at my father's apartment in Arlington before spending another night in Gazebo Park. Although I hadn't seen him during the year I lived with Melanie, I was certain that eleven Mexican beers would temper his mood and save me from an ugly reproach. I arrived at his apartment an hour later. He lived in a two bedroom, one bathroom flat on the third floor of a six building complex called Washington Gardens. It was a depressed, decaying community that I hoped never to revisit. Large rheumatic pin oaks, for example, loomed drearily over flattened grass and never produced enough shade; their network of leafless branches tapped miserably against each other like a pair of poorly fitted dentures. A wrought iron fence stretched tightly around the apartments like a medieval corset and made the entire complex resemble a garrison of poverty. I followed the sidewalk and sidestepped a garbage pile that oozed pink swill onto the hot, pitted asphalt.

As I approached my father's building, I heard a Beethoven piano trio through a set of opened windows; it was his favorite recording. The cello was mournful, the piano sounded hard and spiteful, and the violin recalled moments of melodrama between him and my stepmother. I walked around the corner and noticed a pile of bricks stacked nearly four feet high beside a well window; I looked up. My father had started repairing brickwork around his windowsill and must have stopped for the evening. He's been a maintenance man at Washington Gardens for nearly twenty years and was evidently still at it.

My father wasn't particularly happy to see me. He invited me in, apologized for the bricks that also littered the living room floor, and sat down on the couch between two beams of construction dust lit by a pair of bright windows. He leaned forward, lowered the volume on the record player, and asked me what I wanted.

I was horrified to see this man become so elderly and fragile within a relatively short period of time. His hairline receded behind soft purple knots that stippled his head like engorged ticks. His dark beard, freckled by strands of white brittle hair, started growing from beneath his eyes and tapered into a sharp point just below the chin. His weathered skin turned yellow and his large gray eyes expressed venomous sarcasm. All of these changes caused my father to resemble an old goat rather than an elderly man.

"I need a shower," I said, "and a change of clothes, too."

He lit a tiparillo, coughed through a cloud of thick smoke, and fell into a fit of laughter. I could smell sweet vermouth behind the veil of smoldering blue tobacco smoke that leaked out of his mouth and nose like factory steam. His insensitive laughter exposed my domestic troubles so I decided not to mention them.

"I donated your shit to the Salvation Army," he said, reaching for the bottle of Noilly Prat hidden under the couch. "Once you left with that older woman," he continued, offering me a sip from the bottle, which I politely refused,

"I didn't think you'd be coming back." He took a short pull of vermouth, cleared his throat, set the bottle onto the coffee table and reclined into the cushions. A haze of white sunlight reflected off the bottle and flickered softly onto his hands, revealing cigar-stained fingers and long, blackened fingernails. "Go and take a shower," he said, "and put on my clean work shirt hanging up behind the door."

I thanked him, handed my father a warm Corona, stood up and walked into the bathroom. After my shower, I returned to the living room, relit a cigar my dad hadn't finished smoking, and opened a beer.

"You know," he began, pointing to the nametag below my left collar, "your grandfather should never have shortened our name when he entered the states." He took a pull of beer and licked foam off his mustache and relit a flattened cigar. "Sappo is obviously more poetic than Sapp," he observed, spitting out a piece of tobacco stuck to the tip of his tongue. "But what the hell," he continued, pushing air through the side of his lips with a burst of spite, "you look like a damn guinea, more than me anyway."

He switched records from Beethoven to Mendelssohn and broached the subject of women. He relived past conquests with animation and detail as he explained the different sexual preferences between red heads, blondes, and brunettes. My father corked the vermouth, dried his lips with the back of his hand, and finally narrowed down the affair onto my stepmother, Lynn, who left him for her previous husband nearly fifteen years ago. He preceded the vexing topic with a gentle, elderly grin that twitched above the corners of his mouth. "My bout with life hasn't been a struggle with confidence," he said, looking down the neck of his beer bottle, "it's been a savage fight recovering my pride."

Gray ambient light unfolded softly into the living room as a warm, late afternoon breeze massaged the stale air with a bouquet of dried tree wood and cut grass. The warm beer managed to dampen my anxiety while the clean shirt lightly pressed against my dry skin, gently cooling it. I was comfortable and finally relaxing among those incoherent thoughts that often precede a restful sleep. My dad arched his back, unbuttoned his pants, and reached for the record player; he lifted the needle and restarted Mendelssohn from the beginning.

"Just on account of youth," he assured me as he opened another beer, "you'll find that pride won't outlive your next sexual conquest." He sat back, reanimated his eyes by rubbing them with the palms of his hands, took a drag from his cigar that burned out several minutes ago, and relit it with a broken match. He chuckled at a passing thought, nodded his head approvingly, and continued the outpour of advice. "Yeah..." he paused, "If I were younger, I'd screw more hoonwhistle than a damn mink."

As he spoke, the weight of fatigue crept upon me like a vicious sickness; it anchored my eyelids together and forced my head to sway inadvertently to the left. Mendelssohn began fading into the background as I imagined a songbird alighting upon the branches of an oak tree beside the balcony. I thought I heard its melody, both tremulous and specific, lifting my spirit and easing my burden with greater facility than the alcohol I was consuming. I awakened a few moments later by the sound of shuffling paper. I opened my eyes and saw my father rooting through a drawer. He pushed it shut, counted through a stack of cash, mumbled something to himself, and sat back down. I was just about to close my eyes again when he started talking.

"I know you're tired," he observed, tapping the cash on the table like a deck of playing cards, "but you can't sleep here." I squinted and watched him take a long, slow pull of vermouth; he belched into his fist then stole a quick sip of beer. "Truth be told," he continued, "I need my space."

I sat up, leaned forward, and took in a deep breath while trying not to yawn.

"Habit has become far more valuable to me than sacrifice,"

he explained, "so take my poker winnings." He handed me the wad and suggested I get out of town to recover. "You have enough money to get on a Greyhound and go south," he said, resolutely. "Motels are cheap in southern Virginia."

He opened another Corona and handed it to me. We sat together in the gray half-light of evening while listening to the rest of Mendelssohn. The string instruments merged together in a chorus of melancholy while the piano attacked my composure with a melody of grief and distress; I began thinking about Melanie.

"To rich, Southern women in taffeta dresses!" shouted my father, tapping his beer bottle against mine. He took a long, loud pull of beer, reached for the record player, lifted the needle, and restarted Mendelssohn from the beginning…

novel{ette}s

Nick Sansone
Valerie Cumming

Never Fight a Crown Fire
Nick Sansone

During my time as a firefighter, I cultivated quick reflexes, which have mostly served me well. Unfortunately, my tongue has never been as fast as my legs and arms. That's why I write. It's a brutal form of self-punishment: a way to turn a critical eye upon myself and say the things I wish I could have said in the moment, but that of course do no good to say now. Now that I'm off fire for good, I have all the time in the world to write and write and torment myself with the fantasy that this all could have gone differently.

It was a mistake in the first place for Davies to appoint me crew boss in his stead. I only had four years' experience. Rimsky, over in Zone A34-10R, had been in charge of his corner of the district for something like three decades, so he got first pick in the seasonal hiring. I didn't know how to fight for my place in the HR line, and by the time I got through the red tape and the mobilization papers, all the other boys had done their hiring and the Forest Service applicant pool for southwest Montana was dried up. Only five names trickled down to me, and only two of those applicants had previous experience on hand crews. I should have walked. Even with five newcomers and the three other returning hires and myself, we fell short of the minimum ten-man squad. I wanted my moment, though, and the area had hardly seen any rain all spring. It was going to be a glorious fire season. I had to tell a white lie on my I-12 forms and absorb the paycheck of one fictitious "Stanley Kowalski" into my department's community fund, but I got my authorization and I got my nine-man crew.

The returning hires—Lana, Biggs, and Smitt—carpooled from Texas and showed up in mid-April, out of shape but otherwise ready. I met them in the parking lot.

"You're squad bosses this year," I informed Biggs and Smitt before they had even stepped out of their truck. Lana was squeezed uncomfortably into the backseat. It was hard to tell with her sitting, but I thought she had grown even taller over the past year.

"What about Beshers?" Biggs asked.

"He's not back this year. You're it for returners," I said.

Biggs clicked off the ignition in his Tahoe. "What are we looking at for new guys?"

"Five."

Lana threw her long legs onto the seat next to her and stretched. "That's nine." Her voice was low and serious. I rarely saw her in anything but her Nomex and helmet, but she would have looked good in a professionally cut skirt suit. I could picture Lana in small glasses with thick black frames and a tense ponytail, though the real Lana had bright red shorts and stubbly, muscular legs. Her hair fell glossy and straight around her shoulders.

"They'll be small squads. I'll divvy them up later. Unpack." I meant it as a welcome, but it came out as an order. Smitt rolled his eyes at me from the passenger's seat and I considered this as I walked back into the work center. I would have to rely on him and Biggs to pick up the slack in our small crew. They weren't ideal squad bosses since they had only joined the district two years ago, but they were responsible and would suffice. Lana had been on the crew for the past three years, but I couldn't have made her a squaddie. A squaddie needs firmness and command just as much as he needs know-how.

The new hires arrived one week later. I shook each man's hand as he arrived, matching him with the name from his application. Gerry Burnside, California; Travis Milton, North Carolina; and the two with previous fire experience: Jeremy

Jackson, Indiana and Wayne Flint, Idaho. They seemed like a typical new crew—undisciplined, young, and rowdy. They'd need fixing, but fixing was my job. As they arrived, I sent them to unpack and waited at the work center for my fifth new arrival: Dylan Marshall from Alabama. His application had been the weakest of the five, and as the day stretched into evening, I wondered if he might not show.

When I could hear the mountain crickets chirping from the underbrush, I knew that I had waited too long for Dylan. I'd have to figure out how to manage an eight-man crew. A new headache with new paperwork and the looming possibility that overhead would just scrap the crew and send us home.

Silencing my worry, I dropped into the bunkhouse to see how the guys were settling in. Smitt, Burnside, and Milton had stripped down to their boxers and were gathered around the table in the common room, playing poker. Jackson and Flint were slumped into one of the saggy couches and were talking with Lana and Biggs. Flint—the boy from Idaho—had showered and was neatly dressed in a button-down flannel and crisp blue jeans. He had put some gel in his spiky brown hair and seemed out of place amidst his colleagues. Red flag.

Everybody but Smitt fell into silence as soon as they saw me. Smitt leisurely finished the anecdote he had been telling— the one about the old woman at the Overland Fire, which through countless retellings had lost any correspondence with truth—and then turned to me with a smirk. I crushed a sudden realization. I should have promoted Lana.

"Everything okay in here?" I asked.

Silence. Finally, Flint—pretty boy—cracked a large-toothed smile and nodded. "Yes, sir."

"We're fine," said Lana. She was wearing the sweat clothes that I supposed she slept in. Her position on the couch had nudged her sweatshirt up and I could see a sliver of her flat, toned abdomen.

"Well, you'll report for duty at 06:00 tomorrow morning. Wear your PT clothes."

"PT?" asked Burnside, one of the poker players. He had vacant red-rimmed eyes and a mane of thin, scraggly brown hair. When he arrived, he had been wearing sandals.

"Physical training," said Biggs. "When are they taking the pack test?" he asked me.

"We'll see. A week, maybe. We've got a lot to do first. I'd get some sleep tonight. It's a busy day tomorrow."

"Do we have Dylan Marshall, yet?"

"No." I stood in silence as they waited for me to elaborate, but what could I have said? "Goodnight, gentlemen. And Lana."

I stepped out into the quiet Montana night and heard Smitt's muffled voice and subsequent laughter behind me. Had he said something to make fun of me? I knew that I could appear stiff sometimes. He'd need watching.

As I walked over to my mud-splattered Jeep in the compound's parking lot, I noticed the low rumble of a running engine. There was a new car in the lot: a dull green station wagon with splotches of rust eaten into it. The one working taillight glowed a sickly maroon. I came up beside it and peeked into the driver's side window. The woman inside was short and slightly overweight. Her shoulder-length black hair was pulled into two tiny pigtails high on her head. Shallow salt-streaks of tears had crusted onto her ruddy cheeks. I waited a moment before rapping on the window.

"Help you, miss?" I said, loudly enough for her to hear me inside the vehicle.

She startled and turned a puffy face to me before rolling down her window. "Am I supposed to be here?"

"I'm about to lock the gates for the night. So, no. What's the trouble?" I noticed a pair of suitcases held shut with fraying duct tape in the backseat.

"I'm Dylan Marshall. I think I'm supposed to be here."

I tried to disguise my astonishment with a cough. Dylan Marshall—the female Dylan Marshall—was no firefighter. Her arms were stumpy, her breathing was heavy, and she had been crying. However, she was my ninth man. If I turned her away, I'd be left with an eight-man crew. The Forest Service would never let that slide; its safety regulations were too rigid. I had to make her feel welcome.

"Oh." I coughed again. "How long have you been sitting out here?"

She must have realized then how bizarre she looked to me, because she shut off the engine, stepped out of her car, and self-consciously wiped a few lingering tears from the corners of her eyes. She extended a meaty hand to me, which I shook.

"I'm sorry I didn't come in to let you know I was here. I just pulled in about ten minutes ago. I happened to get a call from my dad right before I got here, so I've been talking to him." She sniffled and laughed a little. "One of 'those' talks, you know?"

"Pull yourself together," I said, which was good advice, but which I should have found another way to say. "Move in as quickly as possible. We start tomorrow at 06:00. We're doing physical training. Welcome."

She smiled and thanked me. I wanted to say something else to her—I'm not sure what—but no words came out, so I turned around without speaking and walked to my Jeep on the other side of the lot. As I drove home that night, I tried to stop thinking about Dylan, but I couldn't. The other new guys seemed alright, but I was worried about her. If a conversation with her father was enough to get her waterworks moving, I wondered about her reaction to a 50,000-acre wildfire—not to mention her reaction to the men on the crew. Firemen are rough around the edges. It's in our nature.

The next morning, I lined my crew out in front of the work center. Everyone but Milton had been right on time. Milton stumbled onto the asphalt walkway that ran between the work center and the bunkhouse at 06:03, his curly red hair gnarled into a ferocious nest, his eyes dulled over from sleep, and his dirty running shoes untied.

"Bad first impression," I warned him. "Fifty push-ups."

The rest of the crew, decked out in workout clothes, counted for him. After thirty-eight, he fell to his knees with a grunt. Jackson—at six and a half feet and at least 250 pounds—bent over and slugged him hard on the shoulder. The others laughed as Milton rose to his feet, rubbing his abused shoulder. I caught Dylan's eye for a moment: her face was twisted into a humorless grin.

"Don't let it happen again," I said. "Smitt, take them out to the Crystal Lake trailhead. Do a five-mile trail run, then some sprint work. Make sure you get their upper bodies, too."

Burnside—the long-haired kid from California—let out a long groan and immediately all eyes were upon him. The tips of his ears turned a deep, embarrassed red.

"Sh," said Biggs.

"Yeah, Hippie," Jackson said, laughing. "Go sit at a desk job if you don't want to work." He turned to the rest of the crew, grandstanding, as they applauded his sentiments. I sought Lana's glance. Pride is almost as dangerous as weakness on the fire line and anybody with experience ought to know it.

"Stop dicking around, guys," Lana said. "Let's do this workout."

Smitt clapped Jackson on the back and said, "Alright, crew. Let's move. You're up front with me, Jackson. The rest of you line out behind him and follow."

As the train of firefighters started a slow warm-up jog to the trailhead at the back of the compound, I grabbed Biggs's arm and motioned for him to remain at the work center with me. When the others were out of sight and earshot, I began to question him.

"How were they at the bunkhouse last night?"

"Alright. Seems like they'll get along. That Jackson kid's pretty funny and Flint's a good guy. They've both got some experience, so they'll probably help hold the crew together."

"Flint?"

"From Idaho."

"Oh, Pretty Boy." I remembered his hair gel from the previous night and hoped that his effeminate tendencies ended there.

"Yeah. The others seem okay."

"We'll watch that Milton kid. Three minutes late this morning."

"He's just got to get used to the lifestyle, that's all. He's really serious about this job, so I know we can straighten him out."

"So, Biggs, what about that Marshall girl?"

"Chunk?"

"Chunk?" I asked. I could guess what he meant, but I wanted to be sure.

"Oh, she's got her nickname already. Like that Burnside kid; they call him 'Hippie.'"

"That didn't take long." Chunk? Fit her to a T. "I guess these names come from Jackson?"

"Jackson and Smitt, yeah."

I was glad that Biggs, without prompting, had brought up the subject I wanted to address. When Smitt left with the crew on their run, he had shot me a superior sneer and muttered something to Jackson. His fierce and animalistic appearance had chilled me. I felt like Smitt was the only one who had the tenacity to call me out on my inexperience. My ability to maintain my authority rested on nobody questioning me. Every glance he threw at me was a suspicious reminder that he knew how new I was and that I couldn't get away with anything.

"How do you think Smitt will do?" I asked.

"He's got a good rapport with the guys. He doesn't like Chunk so much. I guess he thinks she's not going to pass the pack test." I nodded, and there was a brief pause. "*Is* she going to pass the pack test, Hodges?"

"That's for me to worry about."

"If she doesn't get her red card, then we're an eight-man crew. We could never get away with being so thin for numbers."

"She'll pass her pack test. Start your jog." I sent Biggs off to haul his 275-pound body down the trail after the rest of the crew and went to the work center after a few cursory pushups. Chunk. When I had seen her in her PT clothes, I had been relieved to notice that she was more muscular than fat. She was built differently from Lana, however. Chunk was short and stumpy and had thick tree-trunk legs, while Lana was lithe and powerful. Chunk's breasts were huge and hung like crude udders over her noticeable paunch. Lana's chest was flat and long. The two would make an interesting pair. If, that was, Chunk passed her pack test.

After I lay out the saws and fire behavior textbooks in the large engine bay and set up some chairs for the crew, I strolled to the back of the compound to watch them roll in. Smitt and Jackson were the first back, racing each other for first place. Smitt put on an inhuman burst of speed twenty feet from the trailhead and just edged out Jackson. The two doubled over, red-faced and laughing, and collapsed to the earth.

"Hey," I said. "Walk it out. You'll cramp."

Jackson jumped to his feet. "Right, chief."

Smitt took a more leisurely route up and a smarmy smile spread across his face. "How was your workout, Hodges?" he asked, eyeing my sweatless face.

"Jackson, grab some pull-ups," I said with a jerk of my head. Once he had gone, I grabbed Smitt by the arm and yanked him close to me. Our faces couldn't have been more than two inches apart. "Look, I've got a lot to do to get these clowns fire-ready, so put your asshole ego in check. You're a squaddie this year. I need you to make things run smoothly."

He was panting from his run and his hot breath gusted onto my face. "Alright," he said, and tugged his arm out of my grasp before following Jackson to the pull-up bars. I wanted to say more, but no words came out.

Lana finished two minutes after Jackson and Smitt, and Pretty Boy, Milton, and Hippie weren't far behind her. The four began stretching together.

"Nice work, guys," Lana said.

"Thanks, Lana," replied Pretty Boy. "It's a switch being back up in the altitude."

"You'll be fine. Remember, Biggs, Smitt, and I all have a week on you new guys."

Burnside let out a long moan as he leaned over to touch his fingers to his toes. "I think that's the most I've ever run."

"You'll be in marathon shape soon," I said. "Where's Dylan?"

The four exchanged guilty, uncertain glances.

"She hung with me till we got to the lake," Burnside offered, "but then fell back."

A flash of heat flooded my chest. "Never leave a crew member behind," I said.

"Hodges, I can run back and find her," Lana said.

"No. Biggs started after you. He'll run into her. But we don't start classroom until everybody's back."

The others had all assembled in front of the work center and stretched out when, eight minutes later, Biggs and Chunk joined us. Biggs came in at a smooth, easy pace, but Chunk was gasping and holding her side. Her round face was bright red and her cheeks pouched out with rasping gulps of air. Tears of exertion had cut through the film of sweat on her face.

"Little Chunk-Chunk just keeps chunking along!" said Jackson with a wide grin.

"Quiet, Jackson," I said. What to say to Chunk?

"Huh, Chunk? Like that workout?" Jackson continued, sharing a smirk with Smitt. Chunk, racked with wheezy coughs, gave no indication of hearing him, which prompted him further. "Come on, baby, *talk* to me!"

"Sh," Lana said. I was having trouble concentrating.

"Sir!" Jackson said to me. "On my old crew, the boss enforced a penalty for lagging behind."

On reflex, I wheeled around to him and brought a firm fist

into the side of his head. He spun over with a surprised grunt and looked back up at me, massaging his bruised cheek. I immediately regretted my outburst.

"Sorry, chief," he said, his face a bright red mask of embarrassment.

"Leave reprimands to me, Jackson," I said, trying not to notice the seven sets of shocked eyes on us. Out of the corner of my eye, I noticed Chunk, red-faced and sweaty, staring at Jackson in open-mouthed surprise, and my voice returned. "That's sixty-one minutes for five miles, Marshall. The crew's been waiting."

"I'm," gasped Chunk between heaves of breath, "sorry."

"Stretch out," I said. "Everybody else, get into the engine bay." The crew clumped and headed to the work center. I stopped them with a holler. "He-e-ey!" I shouted, my authority restored. "On this crew, we go orderly. Line out behind Lana, and step smart."

They followed my order. Smitt turned to me and shook his head sadly. *"What?"* I mouthed to him before he turned away and followed the others. I brought my attention back to Chunk, who was in an awkward hurdler's stretch.

"You know you've got a pack test to pass, right?"

She nodded.

"I can do it," she said with surprising confidence. "I'm not used to the altitude."

"Get used to it. The pack test is three miles in under forty-five minutes, with forty-five pounds on your back. Uphill. Doesn't sound like much, but when you factor in the weight of your pack and the difficulty of the terrain, you can't be dicking around."

"Yes, sir," she said.

"All right. Finish stretching, then hydrate and give me another five miles."

She flinched and nodded again. "Yes, sir."

With a nod, I walked into the work center to begin training the crew.

. . .

The next week went quickly and smoothly. Milton proved to be a killer sawyer with spot-on accuracy. He was never late to an appointment after the first day. Hippie quickly got acclimated to the altitude and was keeping up with Jackson and Smitt during PT by the weekend. Chunk stayed quiet, but nobody hassled her. Her speed picked up: she was still the slowest person on the crew, but she could get down six miles in fifty-three minutes. Pretty Boy was quiet, too, but a hard worker and always respectful. Jackson grew into his role as class clown and he and Smitt were inseparable by the end of two days. Biggs, Smitt, and Lana helped me keep them all in line and ran some of the demonstrations for me. Nobody forgot that I had punched Jackson, but nobody mentioned it.

On the evening before the pack test, I stopped by the bunkhouse. Smitt and Jackson were smacking each other with pillows. Hippie and Milton were sitting on the floor, chatting and laughing. The others were watching a hockey game on TV. Chunk was lying on the floor in front of the television, doing sit-ups. She had crude red "A"s painted on her cheeks.

"'A' for 'adultery,' Chunk?" I asked from the door.

She grunted and glanced at me with a confident smile. "'A's' for Alabama, Hodges. It's my team." She thrust a thumbs-up at me and turned her focus back to her exercise.

"Okay, guys," I said, louder, "pack test's tomorrow. Line out at the trailhead, stretched and ready to go at 05:45."

Jackson put down the pillow he had been brandishing, and asked, "Anyone want to challenge the PT champion tomorrow?"

"Jackson, it's not a contest. As long as you finish under forty-five minutes, you get your red card. Pace yourselves. Forty-five pounds is more weight than you realize," I said.

"I'm gonna finish in thirty-five, chief," he said.

"Fine."

"Jackson, don't be a dumbass," Biggs said.

I nodded at Biggs and continued. "If you all pass—and I think you will—then we can go on the dispatch boards. We could be on a fire in as few as two days, so get your shit together. All of Wyoming is burning."

The room burst out in a collective whoop. Smitt shoved Jackson with a chuckle, and Pretty Boy high-fived Chunk. Even Lana—who had probably seen more fire than the rest of us—smiled subtly. I couldn't help smiling a little myself. I hadn't been on a fire for almost a year.

When everyone had calmed, I finished. "Get to bed. 05:45 comes early. Lana, see me outside." I jerked my head to her and shut the door behind me. Through the bunkhouse walls, I could hear Jackson yell, "Someone's getting some ass to*night*!" and Lana tell him to fuck off.

She joined me in front of the bunkhouse and we began walking towards the work center. I had already set up the packs with forty-five pound weights inside them that afternoon and they were lined up by the trailhead.

"What's up?" Lana asked. She always seemed uncomfortable when we were alone together. The moon was bright enough that I could see her clearly. I was a couple of inches shorter than her and I found myself looking straight ahead of me as I talked, so that I could avoid having to look up to her.

"How's Chunk doing?"

Surprise registered in her voice. "Fine, why?"

"I don't think she's going to pass."

Lana hesitated. "She might."

"She's really slow, Lana. She's a good hiker, but she can't handle that kind of weight."

"So, if she can't, we'll send her home."

"We're already operating at nine. We can't take another hit, or the whole crew has to disband."

Lana acknowledged the fact with a nod. "What do you

want me to say, then? She might pass. She cut eight minutes off her six-mile time in a week. I've never seen anybody do that before. She's really an animal, and she wants to do this work."

"Wanting isn't enough."

"Fine, so we're fucked," Lana snapped. "Let's just disband tonight, Hodges. What do you want from me? I'm not even a squaddie." There it was, for the first time. That resentment.

"Yes, Lana, Smitt was a mistake. But I can't demote him, or he'll walk, and there goes our crew. I have to have everyone on board."

"You shouldn't have punched Jackson. You might have had Smitt otherwise."

"Shit happens. Is Smitt being alright to her?"

"Yeah. She's fitting in fine. You know, guys are guys, but she's tough."

"She doesn't seem tough."

"Why not?"

I told her about my first encounter with Dylan and she listened quietly before saying, "Hodges, her brother just died. So, yes, she's sad, but it's not like she can't handle the hazing."

"Oh. I didn't know her brother died." We had reached the trailhead by this point and I picked up a pack from the end of the row. "Hey, try this on."

Lana slipped the weighted pack onto her muscular shoulders and snapped the waist belt together. She bounced it up and down on her back and then took it off, placing it back in line.

"What do you think?" I asked.

"It's a forty-five pound pack. What am I supposed to think?"

"Open it."

She unclipped the top flap of the pack and loosened the drawstring. She pulled out the thirty-five pound weight that I had placed inside. She nodded, replaced the weight, and then stood up.

"No," she said.

"It's the only way I can be confident."

"Those regulations are in place for a reason. Safety first, Hodges. What happens when she's actually on a fire? Are you going to carry her to the safety zone if there's a flare up? She'll slow up her squad and put herself in danger. You're willing to risk that, just to make sure you have a job?"

"To make sure we *all* have jobs. The girl is an animal. Maybe she's not in shape yet, but she will be by the time we get on a fire. I thought you'd understand."

"Because I'm a woman?"

"Yes."

"Because I know that women need handouts from asshole guys?"

"This isn't a man-woman thing."

Lana shook her head at me and started back to the bunkhouse. Before going ten yards, however, she turned back to me and said, "You're as bad as Smitt."

. . .

I should have listened to Lana and replaced the weight with a forty-five pounder, but I couldn't bring myself to risk Chunk's failure. Depending on how the summer went, I might get the position permanently. Besides, I wanted it for Chunk. Fire is not an easy field for women to break into, and she was a hard worker. It was in my power to give her an accomplishment, and that in spite of her sex.

I didn't increase the weight in her pack, and she easily passed at 42:03, only a minute and a half behind Pretty Boy Flint. Hippie surprised everybody by finishing in 33:22—well ahead of even Smitt and Jackson, who missed his goal of thirty-five minutes by a minute and ten seconds. I was guiltily satisfied by his failure. Lana finished in thirty-nine minutes flat and didn't accept my congratulations. She waited tensely at the trailhead to watch for Chunk. When Chunk finished, full of exhausted pride, Lana wrapped her in a hug while I removed her pack and quickly shuffled it into the stack. I met Lana's eyes over Chunk's shoulder and they expressed forgiveness. She had seen the victorious tears on Chunk's face and her attitude softened towards me from then on. We were shaky allies once again.

The call from Gibbons down in Shoshone National Forest came as I was printing the red cards for my newly official crew.

"Hodges," he said, "how's the new crew boss?"

"I'm hanging in there."

"Well, you might've heard we're in trouble down here. Our Hedgestone Fire's been bumped up to a Class B. We're pulling resources from Northern Colorado and Cody, and the Redmond Hotshots are lending a hand, too. How'd you like to grow some hair on that newbie chest of yours?"

We loaded up two radios, six cubees of water, two saws, two pulaskis, two McLeods, two shovels, and a combi, and left for Wyoming the next day.

I made the squad decisions as I was leading the caravan to the incident site. I knew that I needed to separate Jackson and Smitt, that I needed to separate Smitt and Chunk, and that I needed to separate Jackson and Chunk. I could not accomplish all three within two squads. Eventually, I decided to give Chunk over to Smitt, but to keep Lana on his crew to keep her eye on him. In any event, it made sense to keep the women together. Chunk and Pretty Boy seemed to get along alright, too, so I grouped him with Smitt as well. That left Jackson, Milton, and Hippie for Biggs's squad. I ran the squad groupings by Lana and Biggs while we were stopped at a gas station.

"Smitt will be pissed that you're giving me Jackson," Biggs said.

"So he'll be pissed," I said.

Lana shrugged. "I'm fine with babysitting your squaddie." There it was again. That anger she usually kept a tight lid on.

I couldn't afford to go into a conflagration with hard feelings, but I didn't have anything conciliatory to say.

"What more can I say, Lana?" I said. "You'll be squaddie next year."

She laughed and shook her head as she got back into her engine. "There's no next year for me, Hodges, at least on this crew."

Biggs smiled knowingly at me and mouthed, *"Women."* I was thankful for the solidarity.

■ ■ ■

We arrived at the Incident Command Center around 13:00 hours and received a briefing from Incident Management. The fire had spread to 7,000 acres and was burning steadily in Type III and IV fuels. Some structures had been lost, and at least forty-eight more houses had been evacuated and were in danger. Weather conditions were eighty-five degrees with a relative humidity of twelve percent. We were advised to spin a weather chain every half-hour to keep abreast of the changing conditions. The fire was approaching the size at which it would begin creating its own wind patterns. Some of the chopper boys had reported frequent torching and occasional spot fires. At the time of that briefing, the fire was approximately twenty percent contained. Our crew was sent to a finger of the main fire that was threatening to make a run down a mountainside into the settled valley below.

I grabbed a pulaski and a radio, gave the other radio to Smitt, and ordered the crew to grab their tools and to line out off of me. We threw on our gear and began the hike up to the fire. As we approached, the sky grew blacker and blacker. A column of ashy smoke billowed furiously from the fire's epicenter and spread across the dusky sky.

"Look at how the smoke plume is bent," I said to Biggs, who was hiking quickly behind me, as I checked the compass dangling from the straps of my fire pack. "Winds are coming from the northwest. Keep your eye on that."

"Copy," said Biggs. He turned to Milton, who was struggling to keep up because of the rocky footing and the huge chainsaw he was humping over his shoulder. "Wind's from the northwest. Pass that back."

As the message went down the line, I picked up my pace. I saw distant flares shooting up into the sky before vanishing into blurry waves of heat. If the fire got into the treetops before we reached it, all hope was lost for the valley we were trying to protect. A firefighter's first rule is that you can't fight a crown fire. You just hightail it to the safety zone and take pictures.

After fifteen minutes of breakneck hiking, I passed a message back to take a three-minute break for hydration. We gathered in a small clearing around a rotten tree stump. The forest had closed in around us—spindly lodgepole pines were clumped closely together, their branches running together in a thick mat of canopy. Crunchy brown pine needles covered the ground. I picked up a needle and snapped it between my fingers. Tinder dry. This blaze was ripping. We could feel hot blasts pulsing towards us from the fire, which was still a quarter of a mile away. The sky was now a dark, uniform gray and a strong campfire smell permeated the air. This was our last stop before going face-to-face with the fire.

"Anyone scared yet?" said Jackson, as he poured a capful of water into his Nomex shirt to wash away some of the sweat he had amassed on the hike.

"Don't waste that, Jackson," said Biggs. "You've only got six quarts."

"Yes, sir," Jackson said, replacing his water bottle.

"Whoever felled this tree didn't line up his face cut right," Milton said, as he sat down on the stump and grabbed a bottle of water from his saddlebags.

I surveyed the crew. They all seemed to be doing okay. Hippie was looking off with a glazed look in his eyes, but I knew to expect that of him. He could pull through when he got down to work. Pretty Boy was breathing hard and a thin line of sweat was running down from his helmet, along his forehead, and into his eyes. I looked over to Chunk and noticed that she was leaning against a tree on the edge of the clearing, her large breasts jerking up and down with labored respiration. Her skin had gone a pale white and her Nomex was saturated with sweat.

"Chunk," I said. Her head lolled to one side as she turned her gaze to me. "How are we doing?"

"I'm," she gasped, "alright." She clearly wasn't used to the weight of her pack. I was irritated by her weakness.

Smitt shot a glance at her and brought his focus back to Jackson, who was waving around the gouging end of his combi and saying that on his old crew they called them "abortions."

"Smitt!" I said. "You need to check on a member of your squad." Smitt made no move. "*Now*," I screamed.

Everybody on the crew grew quiet and averted their eyes, except for Smitt and Jackson whose frosty glares held me in a vise. The whoosh of a torching tree nearby filled the silence. The heat was building, and I knew we had to press on, but Smitt was still staring at me.

I lowered my voice again to a deadly calm. "Smitt. Would you care to check in with your crew member so that we can get to the fire?" Without averting his eyes from me, Smitt lifted his head, opened his mouth, and hacked up a mouthful of phlegm, which he spit onto the forest floor. He grinned, mock-amiably, and challenged me with his raised eyebrows and tense jaw. The low roar of fire was growing louder and I knew that this battle needed to be settled abruptly. I grabbed Smitt by the neck and threw him to the ground. Jackson, shocked into action, instinctually raised his fist, but I put up my hands in a gesture of peace and backed away. Smitt made a low gurgling noise and spit onto the ground as he lifted himself to his knees. Jackson helped him to stand.

"Follow orders," I said, and turned my back on him.

Raising my voice in a general command, I said, "Break's up. Line out off of me by squad. I'll brief you when we reach our anchor point."

I led them out of the clearing at a fast pace. I was still steaming with anger towards Smitt and clambering over the crumbling mountain face helped alleviate my fury. I checked back occasionally to make sure that Biggs was still behind me, but he was fueled with as much adrenaline as I was. The fire was creeping steadily towards us, so I decided to approach it laterally. We could use a patch of already burnt forest as our safety zone, as long as we were careful to watch out for sudden wind shifts that might knock over burnt-through snags.

Ten more minutes of hiking finally brought us to the east edge of the fire. The air was heavy and white-hot embers drifted around us like snow. Heat blasted us from all directions. I could feel myself slowly baking inside my long-sleeved Nomex, gloves, and three-pound fire helmet. Low orange flames twisted along the ground, occasionally leaping into the air with sharp snaps.

I lined out the crew in a large patch of burnt land. Blackened skeletons of trees punctured the carpet of dark grey ash that lined the forest floor. Occasionally a fried branch tumbled, smoking, from the upper tree crowns and brought up a cloud of hot dust. I walked up and down the line, examining the faces of the crew members for any signs of fear, but all I saw was excitement, exhaustion, and determination. Even Smitt looked ready to forget everything for the sake of getting at the fire. Chunk, while still breathing hard, had a set jaw and steely gaze that were almost becoming.

"Guys," I said, "this is our safety zone. If the weather conditions change or the fire gets into the treetops, I will give your squad bosses the signal to return here immediately. To get here, follow your hand line. Be sure to dig your line all the way down to mineral soil. Let's make it eighteen inches thick and direct. We don't want this sucker spotting across our line. Be sure to stay directly next to the fire. If you let any unburned fuel get between you and the main fire, that's your funeral. Squad Alpha—Smitt's guys—you'll attack from the uphill, and Squad Beta, you take the downhill. I'll go with Beta, but I'm on the radio, channel five." I gave Smitt a chance to set his radio to the correct frequency before continuing. I wanted to keep an eye on him, but I knew that it would take two well-functioning squads to bring this fire to its knees, and things would move more expediently if I kept my distance from him. We couldn't waste any more time fighting. "Lana, you'll spin a weather every fifteen minutes and broadcast on channel five as well. Let's anchor off the big rock at my ten o'clock. Any questions?"

There were none, and so I marched the crew to our anchor point. Biggs' squad lined out behind me as I began to follow the fire's perimeter downhill, hacking through the flaming duff and roots at my feet with my pulaski; Smitt's squad disappeared up an incline, doing the same. As soon as my arms were set into their powerful swinging motion, the routine came back to me. Swing, dig, grunt, breathe, step; swing, dig, grunt, breathe, step; swing, dig, grunt, breathe, step. The soil was rocky, and I had to put in some muscle power to get through the thicker roots, but the fire was well behaved and stayed at chest height. The weight of my pack wrenched the sweat out of my back and I was sucking in so much smoke that I had to turn away wheezing from time to time. I was careful to keep checking the back of the line to ensure sure that our whole squad was still hanging on. I idly wondered how things were going on Smitt's squad. If there were any problems, Smitt had instructions to radio me.

We dug in silence for an hour before I called a water break and told the squad to get off their feet for a minute. I smiled at the boys. Told them they'd worked really hard and that, at this rate, we'd be tying in with Squad Alpha before sundown. I plunked down on my pack in the middle of our dugout line and gulped nearly half a quart of water in one swig. The job was running easily and the warmth of the fire on my back felt oddly good. I was home again, in my element, doing the part of my job that I enjoyed most.

"Jackson," I muttered to him, so nobody else could hear, as I wiped my dirty leather work glove across my face, "you're doing good."

He looked up in surprise. "Thanks, chief," he said. "It's good to finally see some action." I smiled at him and he smiled back. Once I got him away from Smitt, the kid wasn't all that bad.

I looked up at the darkening sky as I pulled out my radio to ask how Squad Alpha was doing. Smitt told me things were peachy on his end, so I took a deep, chalky breath of smoky air and tried to relax.

When we started digging again, I allowed the pace to slacken off a little bit. It had been a hard hike in, so I didn't want the boys to overexert themselves. If the fire remained calm, we could afford a bit of time. As the afternoon wore on, the chest-high flames dwindled to knee-high flames, which then dwindled to ankle-high flames.

"Pretty pathetic fire," said Milton. There hadn't been much need for a saw, so he had been felling some of the more hazardous snags in the area the fire had already burned through.

"How's Smitt doing?" asked Jackson, leaning on his combi.

"Keep working," said Biggs. "These things can flare up at any time."

I seconded Biggs' order, but Jackson's question seemed valid. When was the last time Lana had read off the weather? I glanced down at my radio, but its screen had gone blank. *Batteries*. The thought flashed into my head and out again. I had forgotten to bring batteries, but that was okay. I could go back for them if need be, but we had dug nearly twenty-three chains of hand line and we were bound to meet up with Squad Alpha soon. Besides, the fire was just creeping pathetically along the ground by this point.

I dug for a few more minutes in silence. The sun was shining and it felt nice to have some light. The smoke cover had been so oppressive all afternoon that I had been having trouble breathing. Sniffing in a gulp of fresh, relatively clean air, I felt it course into my lungs, pure and smooth.

"Hodges, can we stop for another water break?" Hippie asked.

"Sure," I said.

"It's nice to see some sun," he said.

"Yeah," I agreed, glancing up at the light gray sky, and thinking that I would go back for batteries at the end of the break. A few fingers of sunlight crept through the diminishing screen of smoke that rested above us. Something seemed odd to me about the picture, however. The smoke had cleared up faster than I had ever seen. It wasn't until I felt a light, insistent breeze tugging on my arms that I turned white and threw my pulaski to the ground.

"*Safety zone, guys!*" I screamed. "Hurry! Hurry!" The others looked at me as though I were out of my mind. I knocked a bottle of water out of Jackson's hands and yanked him to his feet. That got them moving. They started at a slow jog, but I kept yelling and pushing them from behind, so eventually I got them into a dead sprint. The whole way I felt an iron knot tightening in my chest. Firefighter's number one tool: *awareness*. Crew boss's number one objective: *the safety of his crew*. If the fire wasn't burning where we were, it was burning somewhere else. The reason we could see daylight was that the smoke column had twisted—the afternoon updrafts were now pushing the fire uphill and directly into Squad Alpha's path.

As we neared the safety zone, I noticed that the flames were taller and more threatening. The heat that had slackened somewhat was back, and it pulsed in waves. Smoke streamed up from the ground, filling the air and gliding uphill with the wind. I looked into the sky. What had previously appeared innocuous was now cut through with lines of black smoke;

while I was watching, a tree about two hundred meters uphill went up in an orange explosion of flame. The upper canopy of the tree flashed white with heat, and a sudden gust of hot air brought its boughs against those of the neighboring tree. There was a brief spark as the fire jumped from one treetop to the next. Before long, the blaze was ripping through treetops, torching vegetation left and right. A fact that I had picked up during my training, four years ago, flashed into my mind: *Fire travels sixteen times faster uphill than down.*

As we scrambled into the blackened-out area that I had designated as our safety zone, I was relieved to notice that Lana, Smitt, and Pretty Boy were safely sitting on their packs under a burnt-out tree. The guys were munching granola bars and breathing heavily. Lana was wracked with tremors. She was bent over her knee with her eyes closed. I could see her lips rapidly moving in prayer. My squad ran over to join the others. Milton and Hippie sprawled out on the ash, their bellies moving up and down with labored breath.

The moment Smitt saw me, he leaped up and barreled directly into me with his shoulder. My solar plexus clenched around my heart, and the wind went out of me as I sprawled onto the ground, landing hard. My helmet flew off. I had barely caught my breath before Smitt was kneeling over me, batting my head with his fists.

"Asshole, asshole, asshole, asshole," he chanted, punctuating each epithet with a ferocious punch. His voice was hoarse, but his fists still had some energy in them. The first three or four strikes shot through me with blinding pain before I grew numb. A thick rivulet of salty, mucousy blood snaked onto my parched upper lip. I could taste metal at the back of my throat. As Smitt kept pummeling, white stars erupted sporadically across my field of vision. I began to think that I might just sink deep into the ashy ground and nap. I heard him saying something, but it sounded as though he were eighty miles away.

I might have blacked out, but the next thing I knew, Smitt

had gotten off of me and was standing apart from the crew, watching the inferno devour the mountainside. It was now a full-on crown fire. Unstoppable. Part of the crew was unsympathetically watching me recover consciousness, and part was staring vacantly at the forest that surrounded us. Nobody, clearly, had anything to say.

I stumbled to my feet, still woozy, and heard Smitt say evenly, "Where's Chunk?"

I rubbed my eyes and counted the group. Eight. Eight. Hm.

"Where's Chunk?" he repeated, louder.

"She was on your crew, Smitt," Biggs said. Now that Smitt had brought it up, everybody snapped to attention. They looked around in puzzlement. Eight people.

"*When you didn't answer your radio,*" Smitt growled, pounding his fist into his other hand, "I sent her back to tell you we were at the safety point."

"By *herself?*" Immediately, I was on my feet. "Lana, how the fuck did you let him do that?"

Lana looked up from her knee and her face was red, sweat-drenched, and furious. "*I don't know,*" she screamed. "*I'm not a fucking squaddie.*"

Looking back, I can see that what I did next was idiotic, but I was still reeling from Smitt's thrashing and, besides, I was disoriented by all of the smoke that the fire was sending off. I lumbered to Lana, thrust my face an inch away from hers, and swiped a flat palm hard across her cheek. Before the others could say or do anything else, I threw off my pack, grabbed a fusee and my fire shelter from the outside pouch, and sprinted off the way I had come.

The fire had swollen into a massive, roaring wall of flames. It had spotted easily over our eighteen-inch hand line and raced across the treetops downhill towards the valley. The settlements we had been charged to protect were not going to survive. I kept low to the ground so that I could minimize the amount of smoke I sucked in. All the same, it filled my throat and nostrils and billowed into my face. As I crept along the forest floor, I yelled: "Chunk-Chunk! Chunk-Chunk!"

A realization struck me: I could die out here. I had never really thought of this before, but I was literally risking my life. The growing heat wouldn't relent. It would keep piercing me and piercing me until, eventually, I had inhaled enough burning gas to singe my lungs and kill me. I looked back the way I had come from. A burning tree had collapsed across the hand line, thus blocking my exit. I could barely see anything farther away than my hand.

Suddenly, I heard a faint yell from somewhere downhill of me. "Help!"

I took a deep breath and charged into the blackness beneath me. Fire lashed at my limbs and toyed with the edges of my Nomex, but I didn't have my pack to weight me, and some divine force must have been with me, because I charged right into Chunk and pinned her to the ground. I grunted in her ear. "Stay down, and try not to breathe."

The fire had hooked around behind us and was now running up the hillside towards us. There was only one thing I could do to save our lives. I broke open the fusee I had brought with me, creating a spark of heat. I dumped the flare into the brush that was just uphill of us and uttered a frantic, silent prayer.

At first it didn't look like the brush would catch, but a low, sprite-like flame began nervously dancing in the undergrowth. Chunk went limp under me; I think she must have passed out, either from smoke inhalation or from exhaustion. I fanned the fire I had just started, trying to feed it with oxygen. We didn't have a lot of time; I could feel myself already getting giddy and light-headed.

Just as I thought I would black out, the fire I had started roared to life and ripped up the mountainside above us. The undergrowth crinkled and twisted in on itself before leaping into miraculous luminescence and disintegrating into hot, fertile ash. Hot, fertile, *safe* ash. As soon as my fire had burned out a two-foot patch, I dragged Chunk into it and blew into her mouth. Our makeshift safety zone wasn't nearly large enough, and I could feel my skin blistering and scorching under the intense heat. Chunk didn't respond to my attempts at resuscitation, so I blew again, and again, and again, and again. The main fire was continuing to burn up to us, but my fire was also spreading quickly. A strip of land about five feet by five feet had been burned out. It wasn't very big, but it might be enough to keep me alive. When the main fire reached our line of ash, it faltered. I cuddled Chunk's body close to mine, praying that our safety zone was large enough. I brought the sleeve of my dirty Nomex across my mouth and Chunk's, using it as a makeshift air filter. With an audible sigh, the fire finally broke and sent two lines of flames around the side of our impromptu safety zone and, not finding an entrance into our protective womb, continued up the mountainside, leaving us with our lives. When I noticed this, I was too concerned to feel relief. I needed to resuscitate Chunk.

Her eyes fluttered open after half an hour. The smoke had cleared somewhat by this point, leaving behind an unearthly gray mist. We were covered, heads to toes, in ash, and the air reeked of campfire. From our position, I could just make out the face of the adjoining valley. The fire was raging there. A town of forty-eight houses, a church, and two supermarkets was being consumed. A helicopter puttered over the settlements three miles away, overlooking their destruction. Failure. I gave Chunk a clumsy pat on the back.

"I almost died," she said.

I couldn't find anything to say to her. "Shhhh," I said, pulling her into me.

"My brother always said I wasn't cut out for men's work." A lone tear trickled through the dirt and ash smudged over her burnt face. I held her as she stared at the hazy sky and the burnt-out forest around us, until we were able to stand up and begin the shameful hike back to base camp.

Chunk quit that evening, and I tendered my resignation directly following. With only a seven-person crew and no boss, the entire crew was demobilized from the fire immediately. Nobody spoke on our drive back to Montana.

I collected the crew's gear back at the work center and sent them all back to their homes. Chunk pulled me aside to thank me for saving her life. It was an obligatory gesture of appreciation. She spoke with a stoniness that I might have expected from a bitter ex-girlfriend. Lana didn't speak. She turned a pitiful eye on me as she stepped into Biggs's truck to head back to Texas. When I waved goodbye, she shook her head and slammed the door. The entire crew had gone by the next afternoon.

Before departing myself, I took a last look at the compound through the chain-link fence. Three engines, four cabinets of hand tools, eight chainsaws, five Shindawa pumps, six-hundred-and-twenty feet of hose, and a dusty heap of bladder bags: none of which would be used until the next summer. I would never, of course, be invited back into the Northern Montana crew.

"Where did I go wrong?" I thought. "Sometimes life just gets away from you, I suppose, and it happens slowly, right under your nose." Rubbing a rough hand over my stubbly chin, I muttered "I'm sorry" into the empty mountain air, knowing that nobody was around to hear.

On June fifteenth, I locked the gates to the compound for the rest of the summer. They say that when an airplane crashes, it is never due to a single cause—that such a disaster occurs as a result of several contingencies all failing in balletic succession. A fire works the same way. Most fires, foiled by unfavorable terrain, lack of fuel, or adverse weather conditions, peter out before reaching a substantial acreage; however, the few fires that manage through dumb luck to slip through every chink in nature and mankind's defenses make headlines. Crowning, they are unstoppable.

I know that there are things I could have done differently,

but it's a cruel quirk of disasters that the inquest can only be made after the smoke has cleared. Perhaps I'd been walking the line of catastrophe from birth but had not been forced to realize it before that summer. Perhaps we are all blithely tottering two steps from ruin. Perhaps we can never know anything until we've been condemned. Or perhaps this is all hollow self-justification. Perhaps I'm just an asshole who made mistakes. But that, I reckon the most probable conclusion, is the least satisfying.

Like New
Valerie Cumming

On the day my mother chose to leave, I spent the afternoon on a mattress in Tony Roger's backyard, smoking and singing along to whatever we could find on the radio. School had only been out a week, but already the heat and humidity were so bad I could hardly stand it. Between songs I let Tony kiss me some, but when he tried to do more than that I pointed at the cars going by on his street and up at the sky, bleached white with heat, and told him that it wasn't a good time. I told him the truth, which was that I was supposed to be home packing for the trip my mother and sister and I were leaving for the next morning. I told him that any minute now my mother would call up looking for me, which wasn't a total lie either, except that if my mother really wanted to find me she'd know where to go without calling. Tony's mother ran a landscaping business, which meant that she was pretty much out of the house all summer. So we spent a lot of time there, Tony and me, and when she was at home we'd borrow her big white windowless van and drive it out to the woods. The back had plenty of space in it once you pushed aside the tools and the bags of mulch and fertilizer, and when things were going well with Tony and me we could spend a whole afternoon in that van without ever coming out for air. But it was summer, and I tended to get tired of Tony in the summer—how his dark mood never changed, the way his long pale legs never seemed to tan no matter how many hours we spent lying in the sun. So I waited until the sun was just beginning to graze the tops of the trees in the yards across the street, and then I kissed Tony one last time and ground my cigarette out in the grass next to all of the others and walked off slowly, carefully, knowing as I did that he was watching me go, that his eyes were on every part of me in ways that his hands were dying to be—if only I would let them.

It took twenty minutes to walk home, to discover that my mother hadn't waited for me to pack and had, instead, just thrown a bunch of my clothes in the backseat without even a suitcase to hold them. I opened the trunk and saw all of my mother and Bridget's things there, in matching train cases and duffel bags stacked neatly next to each other. I went inside and there were the two of them, eating sandwiches at the kitchen table just as if nothing were out of the ordinary. My mother pushed away her sandwich when she saw me. She covered it with a napkin with one hand and ground out her cigarette on the edge of her plate with the other and said, "Good, you're home." Which meant: "Let's get a move on."

Bridget was sitting at the table still, her head swinging like some dumb pendulum, back and forth, between my mother and me. I said, "But we're not leaving until tomorrow."

"Change of plans," she said. She got up to dump her uneaten sandwich in the sink.

My mother, when she wanted to, could be really beautiful. But this wasn't one of those days. Her blonde hair was limp, her face lined and exhausted, looking like she'd been sitting at the kitchen table smoking cigarettes since morning, which maybe she had. I watched Bridget gather her purse and her jacket from the table and stand up. "What?" I said, "You're just going to follow whatever insane order she dishes out? We didn't even get to say goodbye to Dad."

Bridget just shrugged, and wouldn't look at me.

I said, "Well, you don't need that jacket, that's for sure. It's hot as balls out there."

She started to put it back on the table. "Take the jacket," my mother said. "Like I told you before, you never know when you might hit on a cold night."

"That's crazy," I said. We were driving to Florida to spend

a week with an old college friend of my mother's while my father stayed in Ohio to work. I'd said more than once that I thought he had the better deal.

For the first few miles, Bridget rode up front next to our mother while I sat in the backseat taking inventory. "You forgot my deodorant," I said, finally. "We'd better stop, because I'll tell you now there's no way I'm using yours."

"We'll stop," my mother said. She was merging onto the highway, her eyes in the rearview mirror, distracted.

"I'll need shorts, too," I said. "You only brought one pair."

"Well, maybe if you'd packed yourself," my mother said. "Like I asked you to."

Just before the bridge that would take us out of town and over the Ohio River into West Virginia, my mother pulled the car to the side of the road and told us that we weren't going back. "Not in a week," she said. "Not ever."

For at least a full minute I thought she was joking, but then I looked at Bridget, who was staring into her lap, twisting her favorite jade ring from my father around and around on her finger, and saw that not only was it true, but it looked like Bridget had known about it all day. I got pissed then, until it occurred to me that Bridget was only twelve and that kids her age had to listen to their mothers. They couldn't help it; they were stupid that way. From the highway you could see the town below, bordered by the river on one side, and beyond that the hills and factories of West Virginia. I was thinking about a joke I'd heard my father tell a million times about leaving your shoes on the bridge so that the West Virginians coming over from the other side would have something to put on their feet, but I couldn't get the wording right in my head. I said, "What about Dad?"

"What about him?" My mother patted Bridget's bare knee, then turned halfway around to face me. I looked out the window. She said, "It's late, and I'm starved. Let's stop for something to eat and then, if it makes you feel better, you can call him from the restaurant."

"I'll do that," I said, still looking out the window. The landscape I knew by heart suddenly looked strange and unfamiliar, like someone had outlined every building and tree in black magic marker. "He'll be there to pick us up in an hour."

She turned forward again, but not before I saw her smile. "Oh, I doubt that."

"Screw you," I said, and braced myself, but she only flinched. Beside her, Bridget looked down at her lap again.

Halfway across the bridge, my mother said, "I'm sorry. That came out wrong. It's just, can you picture him? Tearing down the highway in his business suit, in search of the children he barely even has time for when they're right in front of his eyes?"

"Sure," I said, hating her, the dirty way the back of her head looked, her hair coming in silvery at the roots.

"Well, then, you know him better than I do," she said, and kept right on driving.

The thing about my mother was that she considered herself a wanderer. "Untamable," she called herself, blaming my father for why we could never move. First she wanted to go to North Carolina, because of the ocean, and then later it was Colorado for the mountains. "It's just a stupid test," she would complain to him, and my dad would slam his fist on the kitchen table as he did every time this topic was mentioned and shout, "Merilee, it's the goddamned *bar* exam. You don't just up and take it. There's a lot of preparation involved."

"Other lawyers move," she complained to her cigarette. "It's not like it's impossible."

"Sure, sure it's not," he said. "How about I spend the next few months at the law library studying, just to find a job as a clerk someplace pretty, making half of what we make now?"

That, the part about the money, shut her up every time. A couple of times in the last year she had disappeared for a day or so, leaving notes on the kitchen table saying she needed "space" or "air," but she was always back for breakfast in the morning. This was the first time that her leaving seemed to be for real. At the Friendly's in Parkersburg, West Virginia, my mother said she had chosen Florida for us because it was warm and because of her friend there, Rhonda, who said we could stay with her as long as we needed to get ourselves set up. When the waiter came, my mother smiled up at him and ordered cheeseburgers and milkshakes and fries for all three of us, even for Bridget, who was a little on the curvy side and perpetually on a diet. "We're in a bit of a hurry," she told the waiter, who couldn't have been much older than I was, but I saw him smile back at her and knew she was pleased. As he walked away she said, "I couldn't breathe back there, girls. I was dying in that house. Can you begin to understand that?"

"I like Ohio," I said. I asked her for the phone card, to call my dad like she had promised me, planning already to tell him all about the waiter.

"Here," she said, shoving her whole purse across the table at me. "Take it."

The payphone was in a smoky vestibule at the front entrance of the store. On the wall were posters listing all the different types of ice cream you could order. I read them all silently to myself while the phone just rang and rang and rang.

When I got back to the table, the food had arrived, but it was pushed off to one side to make room for the travel booklets and maps that my mother and Bridget had spread across the table. They were bent over looking at them, their heads so close together they were practically touching. I waited for either of them to ask me about Dad, but they didn't say anything. Finally I pointed at the booklets and said, "So what's all this?"

"I thought since we were driving, we might as well take our time," my mother said. She'd lit a cigarette and was smiling. The food and the colorful books full of beautiful places seemed to have improved her mood. "We're not exactly in a hurry, and there's so much to see."

"For you, maybe," I said, pouring ketchup all over my fries in a way I knew my mother thought was disgusting. I licked my fingers. "I wish you'd stop saying 'we.' One way or another, I'll get home. What you're doing is kidnapping, you know."

"Well, Bridget and me, then," she said. When the waiter came by to check on us, my mother winked and asked to borrow a pen, and then she and Bridget went through the book, circling things they wanted to see. From all they circled, it didn't look like they would get to Florida before Christmas. "There're some underground caves a few hours south of here," my mother said, nibbling at her hamburger, getting a smear of mustard across her lip. I didn't tell her about it. She said, "Indian tribes used them to hide out in. That might be interesting."

I remembered the poster I saw in the lobby. "I'm going to want ice cream," I said. "This place is famous for its ice cream."

I waited for her to point out that I'd already had a milkshake, but she didn't. She just waved her hand without even looking at me and said, "Fine, fine, we'll all have ice cream. After all, we have to celebrate."

"Celebrate what?" I asked.

"Freedom."

I snorted. She called the waiter over again and asked him to put three single scoops of chocolate on the bill. I told her to make mine a double and she said, "Whatever," like she was so tired of me, she couldn't even argue anymore.

In the ladies' room with Bridget, the two of us washing our hands after dessert, I said, "You don't have to do this, you know."

I expected Bridget to say *Do what?* or some other dumb thing, but instead she dried her hands very carefully on a paper towel and said, "I know."

"Just because she's our mother doesn't mean we have to go along with whatever crazy scheme she's cooked up, you know. You could come home with me instead."

"Is Dad coming for you?" Bridget asked. In the mirror over the dirty soap-scummed sink, her eyes met mine. Usually, I'm the one closest with Mom, and a part of me wondered if Bridget was just enjoying the sudden reversal of roles.

"Maybe, maybe not," I told her. "But if he doesn't, there's always Tony. He'll come for us in his mother's big white van, so there's room for us all."

"I don't want to sit in back with all of those rakes and mulch and shit," Bridget said, crumpling her paper towel and throwing it away.

"So you'll sit up front," I lied. "Don't be an asshole."

"I'll think about it," Bridget said. She walked out of the restroom and back to our table, and there was nothing for me to do but follow her.

After that, it was my turn to ride up front, but I refused to navigate or in any way contribute to what was happening, so my mother kept drumming her nails on the steering wheel and sighing, and I could tell she was just dying for it to be Bridget's turn in the front again. Instead of looking at the maps, I busied myself looking out the window at the dark hills and thinking about what was ahead. I could count the things I knew about Florida on one hand. There were beaches and hurricanes, and a friend of mine had gone on vacation there once and said they had flea markets where people sold baby alligators in aquariums and T-shirts with Confederate flags on the fronts of them. I tried to conjure up a mental image of my mother's friend Rhonda, someone from college who had come to dinner a couple of times when Bridget and I were kids, but all I could remember was that she was on the fat side, with huge boobs and a necklace with a cross on it that hung right down into her cleavage, and she looked at my father a lot and laughed too hard at jokes he made that weren't very funny. I said to my mother, "I hope you've thought all of this out better than I think you have." She didn't say anything back, which I took to mean that maybe she hadn't.

After another hour of driving south, my mother found a Holiday Inn. She pulled into the parking lot. "Let's stop here," she said, turning herself half around so she could smile at Bridget in the back seat. "What do you say we splurge a little, have a good night's sleep? In the morning, we'll have some breakfast and feel like new again."

It was late, but not that late. The outdoor pool was already closed, but through the glass doors you could see the indoor pool was all lit up and empty except for a couple of kids who were still splashing around in the shallow end and their parents, who were busy sitting on a couple of lawn chairs looking bored. It seemed like a nice enough place, but I didn't want to say that. Instead I said, "Maybe you'd better save your money. You should try planning ahead a little."

My mother turned back around in her seat so that both hands were on the steering wheel. She said quietly, "Sooner or later you're going to have to stop being so angry at me."

"Maybe I do, maybe I don't," I said. "It wasn't like I had a choice in any of this."

"You still need me, you know," she said then. It was almost a whisper.

"Like hell I do."

I waited in the car while my mother and Bridget went in to see about a room. I was thinking about Florida again, imagining white sand beaches and the bluest blue waves. I imagined Tony and me backing that old white van right up to the water and opening the back doors up to all of that blue. Then my mother knocked on my window. "Are you coming?" she said, like she thought I might spend the whole night out in the car, like she didn't have any idea what to expect from me anymore.

Inside was like a palace. Lots of tile, plush couches, tiny tables with vases of fresh flowers everywhere. We had stayed at hotels before on vacation, but they were usually just small, squat places with rooms that opened onto the parking lot and a square pool with chipping paint and leaves floating on top—not because we were poor, but because my father believed in making good time, which required not getting too comfortable anyplace along the road. My mother had the room key in her hand but she was taking forever to leave the lobby, stopping at each of the vases and sniffing in this deep way that was really embarrassing. My mother has a thing about flowers. At home she was always working in the garden, which I supposed was one of the reasons why she had chosen Florida as her new residence: someplace warm and blooming all year round. Bridget must have been thinking the same thing I was, because in the elevator she said to mom, "I bet he'll send you flowers. What will you do if he sends you flowers?"

My mother was studying the elevator buttons like she was having trouble reading the numbers on them and said, "I don't know. Send them back, I guess."

"You can't do that," I said. "It's not like a letter. You can't just write 'Refused' across a bouquet and leave it in the mailbox to get picked up."

"Then I guess I would have to keep them," my mother said, sounding more tired than I'd ever heard her before in my life.

The room was okay—two double beds, a desk with the usual hotel stationery, the bolted-down TVs in the armoire, the same old garish watercolors above bright paisley bedspreads. It had that hotel room smell, though: clean and stale at the same time, the kind of clean that immediately reminded you of the hundreds of people who had stayed in this room before you. It was late, but not too late, so my mother unpacked her train case and then announced that she was going for a walk. "Just to get the lay of the land," she said, and it was clear she wasn't inviting us along. "And please, girls, no room service."

The first thing I did when she was gone was pick up the phone to try to call my father, but the front desk hadn't unlocked our phone, so then there was nothing to do but sit. Bridget flipped channels with the remote until she found some soft-core cable-TV thing that was mostly just boobs and moaning. I was feeling restless from so many hours pent up in the car. I thought for a minute about writing Tony a letter on the hotel stationery, but didn't know what I'd say, so I stood up and wandered around the room awhile. Finally I remembered my mother's makeup in the bathroom and said, "Come on, Bridge, we're going out."

One good thing about Bridget is that she doesn't talk much, but she doesn't argue much either. She has my dad's coloring but her face is my mother's, everyone says so, which means that she can be beautiful when she wants to be. In the Holiday Inn bathroom she stood still and let me do her face, and when I was done she looked twenty instead of barely twelve. She had boobs, too, which was unfair because even though I was four years older I didn't have much to speak of in that department, which just goes to show that life isn't fair and that some people have all of the luck. I got Bridget ready, and then I got myself ready, and then we grabbed the extra room key from the nightstand where my mother had left it and took the elevator downstairs to the lobby, looking, as my father would have said if he'd been there to see us, for trouble.

The only place open in the hotel was this sleazy little bar called Memories, the kind of place where you knew men on business trips were always going to see if they could pick someone up. We went inside, me pulling Bridget along by the hand like some lost little kid, and, just as I expected, there were three guys in suits sitting at the bar drinking while a trampy-looking waitress with tight jeans and big, puffy blonde hair stood there talking to them. It was also karaoke night, according to the sign on the door, which meant that a bunch of people were sitting at tables half-watching while a group of frat boys belted out some drunken rendition of "You've Lost That Lovin' Feelin'," laughing and slobbering all over each other. I pulled Bridget over to a booth in back and sat down. When the waitress came over, I ordered us two Cokes with lemon, and since we didn't have any money I just showed her my key and told her to charge it to the room, and she seemed fine with that. Bridget and I were looking good, all made up, and it seemed like the kind of place where we might have been able to get away with it, but I didn't want to risk ordering beers and getting caught and chewed out by some pimply night manager. So Bridget and I just sat and sipped our Cokes and watched one lonely person after another humiliate themselves at the microphone. The frat boys were okay, but as it got later and people got drunker a whole string of women got up, each one dressed kind of like the waitress, singing these sad country songs like "Jolene," and it was funny for a while, but after that it just got sort of depressing. I could tell that Bridget felt the same from the way she was just staring into her Coke, twirling the lemon around and around with her straw, not saying much or even smiling. I almost felt guilty for bringing her along, until I remembered that none of this was my idea in the first place and that at least I hadn't run off on her tonight the way my mother had.

To make conversation, I asked Bridget what she was thinking about. She looked at her Coke and said, "Nothing." I was thinking about something my mother had said in the car, something about how my bad attitude was actually her fault. She was talking about the road trips she and my dad took to Canada and California before Bridge and I were born, and she said, "If only we had shown you something of the world, maybe you would know what you've been missing." I thought about how this bar was the perfect example of how wrong she was; it seemed to me that the same aimless loneliness existed no matter what state or province or country you were in, that no matter how far you tried to drive to escape it, it was always there waiting for you on the other side.

After a while, the frat boys began sending drinks over to our table. The waitress brought them, not even bothering to ask for ID. She lined them up carefully across the center of the table, wine coolers and rum-and-Cokes, the kind of drinks the boys must have thought girls our age would go for, not that they even knew how old we really were. I didn't bother looking up or waving to say thank-you, even though a couple of the boys were cute enough. I just sat back and watched Bridget take little sips from the glasses one by one, making faces after each drink, getting drunk for what was probably the first time in her life. She was quiet at first, but then the red in her lips spread across her cheeks and forehead and she started smiling a lot more than she had before. She even waved once at the table of boys, even though I told her not to, even though I warned her that was the kind of thing that could get you raped or killed or worse. Bridget and my mother were both dumb in the same way about men. They both believed that there was a soul mate for everyone, that it was just a matter of finding him. Consequently, a woman could never rule out anyone, because you never knew when your soul mate was just around the corner. He could be a horny frat boy in a bar or a lonely businessman or a homeless guy on the banks of the Ohio; it didn't make any difference. I thought they were both nuts. I was sixteen and already had dated enough by then to know that every boy can be your soul mate for a while.

So it was because of Bridget, not me, that these boys started coming up to our table, half-walking, half-dancing to us, the same stupid grin on each of their faces. They motioned at us to scoot over in the booth, and Bridget did, but I stayed right where I was. "Get lost," I said to the tallest of the boys, the one who seemed to be their leader.

They made these loud, laughing, whooping noises then, which let me know that my telling them to get lost was perfectly expected, like the first step in a dance. They leaned their blue-jeaned hips against the table and asked if we were from around here.

"Not really," I said. "Why do you want to know?"

"No reason." That was the tallest one. The others, his friends, seemed content to just keep standing there smiling. "Look," he said then, "a bunch of us are going down to the pool, and we wanted to know if you two ladies would like to join us."

"The pool's closed," I told him.

"Not to us."

"I want to sing," Bridget said. It was one of the first things she'd said all night. We all watched her push out of the booth and go stand in line with the rest of the women waiting for their number, wobbling a little as she crossed the floor. Then the boy, the tall one, slid into her spot in the booth.

"Look," he said, leaning so close that I could feel his breath tickling my face. "This place is way too pathetic for two gorgeous girls like yourselves. Let's get out of here."

"I have a boyfriend," I said, which was sort of a lie because Tony was a lot of things to me but was not officially my boyfriend.

"Not tonight," the boy said, looking straight into my face as he said it. And I can't deny it; something about the intense way he was looking at me made my heart jump up into my throat and then sink down low into my belly, and there was a moment, just a moment, when I thought about what it might be like to follow these boys home to their dorm or apartment or whatever, to forget all about my mother and maybe even Bridget until morning, when I could call my dad or Tony or whoever and have them come and pick me up. Or maybe the tall boy would drive me home, and we would never see each other again, but I would always remember this shitty bar and how nice he had been to drive me all that way. Something about the warm night and the alcohol made it almost possible to believe these things could be true, just for a minute. Then I got real and said, as clearly as I could, "Forget about it."

"Okay, sure," the boy said. He leaned back against the wall, stretching his legs out across the booth, and offered me a cigarette.

I shook my head. "I'm serious," I said. "I have to look out for my sister."

He turned halfway around to look at the makeshift dance floor/stage, where Bridget was just taking the mike from the woman in front of her who had been singing "Wind Beneath My Wings" in this heartfelt way that let you know she didn't think the lyrics were a huge joke. The guy said, "Looks like your sister can take care of herself."

"She's twelve," I said, and the guys laughed and the tall one blew curls of cigarette smoke out his nose and said, "Yeah, right."

The thing about Bridget was, she could sing. She'd never had lessons or anything; she just had a talent for it. She'd chosen some old Elton John song, and even though the song itself was shitty, even though she was obviously drunk, the way she sang it made every single person in the bar stop and look at her. When she was done, no one clapped; there was a moment of silence while Bridget handed the microphone to the woman behind her in line, and then the music started up again and all the normal bar noises, the laughter and clinking of glasses, came flooding right back, and that perfect moment of stillness—the memory of Bridget's last flawless note hanging like an echo in the smoke-thick air—was gone forever.

After that the boys took off, which I had known they would do. Something about Bridget was shining now, and some of that shine managed to rub off on me until we were no longer just two teenaged girls in a bar; there was something almost sublime about us. Boys, I had learned, didn't like that. They liked you as plain and un-shining as possible, so they could paint over you like a mural with whatever it was they wanted you to be. I thought about explaining all of this to Bridget, but she was clearly too far gone to listen, so instead I took her by the hand and led her away from the bar and down the back staircase to the outdoor pool, which was so perfectly flat and black in the darkness that it could have been bottomless. I thought it would be good for her to get some air. As I had suspected, the boys had chickened out and were nowhere to be seen. There was no fence or gate around the pool, just a sign posting the hours and a warning not to swim when the lifeguard was off duty—the empty chair lurking there over us like some kind of beacon of doom. We sat down and put our feet in the water, which was freezing despite the hot West Virginia night. I could tell it was sobering Bridge up a little. She was staring at the water and some of the glow was fading away, and she was beginning to look like the same old Bridget again. I sat close to her, half-afraid she was going to pitch forward right into the pool, and said, "You know, you were good back there. You should take some lessons or something. You'd be really amazing."

She shrugged. She said, "I wish those boys hadn't left. I was having fun."

Something about the way she said that, when I'd done all I could to get rid of the guys, mostly for her protection, pissed me off. I said, "You know, you and Mom really need to get smarter about men. I'm going to have to follow the two of you to Florida just to make sure you don't get yourselves killed."

We were quiet for a long time after that, just splashing our feet a little in the water. I was beginning to think Bridget hadn't heard me when she finally said, "I don't understand why you're fighting so hard to keep Mom from being happy."

"Because it's crazy," I said. "Happy, running away, searching for the perfect man? What happens when he doesn't turn up in Florida either? Do you move again? Does she go running back to Dad?" In the dark, even close up, it was hard to read Bridget's face. I said, "I thought you and Dad were supposed to be so close or whatever. Do you ever even think about what he must be feeling right now?"

She nodded and looked away from me. "We always knew she was going to leave," she said to the water. "I guess I'm just grateful she wants to take us with her."

I didn't know what to say to that. I was angry, at my

mother first of all, and at Bridget too, for being so young and so full of need. So I said, "Sure, but what about you? Your school, your friends?"

Bridget shrugged. She didn't have to remind me that she didn't have many friends; I already knew that. I was popular enough, though I respected Bridget for being a bit of a loner. Sometimes friends want to keep you like a blank wall the same way that boys do. She said, "I think she's brave."

"Brave?" I laughed. I almost stood up and went back inside—it sounded that ridiculous—if it hadn't been for the fact that Bridget probably would have fallen in and drowned the second I left. I said, "Brave, to run away?"

"Brave, to go after what she wants," Bridget said.

I couldn't help it; when she said that I started thinking about those women in the bar, wearing too much makeup and too-tight jeans, belting out songs about lost love just as if they were alone in their own apartments, and I thought, Well, at least Mom isn't one of them. I wouldn't say that I was impressed with her right then, but maybe I could see a little of where Bridget was coming from. To make peace, I asked her if she wanted to get in the pool. "I don't have my bathing suit," she said.

"Neither do I," I told her. "Who's gonna know?"

We looked around at all of the windows surrounding the courtyard. It was late, but half of them were still lit, though covered with curtains. Still, all of those windows, like eyes looking down at us, were enough to make me shy. I made like I was going to pull my shirt up over my head, then said, "Actually, it feels a little cold" and sat down on the pavement again next to Bridget, watching her lift her legs one at a time over the surface, water dripping from her pink-painted toenails like tears.

After a while, Bridget said, "She won't really go without you, you know," and I had to pretend hard not to hear her.

I think we might have sat there all night, just dunking our feet in the water and not talking, except that my mother came looking for us. If she noticed that Bridget had been drinking, she didn't say so. She just stood at the side of the pool with her arms crossed over her chest and said, to both of us, "I was worried about you."

"Well, you didn't have to be," I said, not looking at her. "We're perfectly fine."

"What have you been up to?" she asked, her voice feigning lightness, but neither of us said anything back. We didn't ask her to sit down. Finally she cleared her throat and said, "I spoke with your father. He says that if either one of you still wants to go back, to put you on a bus in the morning and he'll pick you up at the station."

"He's not coming himself?" I asked.

"Well, he might. I don't know. I didn't ask him to. I just said you wanted to go home, and that's what he told me to do."

I said, "Did he sound lonely? Was he mad at you for running off like this?"

My mother stopped waiting for us to ask her to sit down and just sat, cross-legged, on the concrete. "He's glad to know you're here, and that you're safe," she said carefully. "Any of the rest, you'll have to ask him about it."

I pictured my father alone in our house, maybe pacing around the living room the way he did when he was late for something and waiting for my mom to get ready so that they could leave. I remembered how, on the hottest Ohio summer days, he would lift up my ponytail and blow gently on the back of my neck to cool me off. But he wasn't coming. I watched my mother stand up and stretch like a cat. The way she moved, it was like someone was always watching her, or like she always hoped someone would be. She said, first to Bridget and then to me, "Are you getting in?"

"No," I said for both of us. Bridget was sitting funny, lilting a little to one side like she wanted to fall over and sleep right there on the concrete. That's when my mother started taking off her clothes. One thing about my mother is that she isn't shy about her body, even though she doesn't have much of a body to speak of. She's thin as a boy, sort of flat-chested, and petite in this way that makes me feel enormous. When I was about eleven, I was at a department store trying on bathing suits with my mother, and she put her hands on my sides and said, "You'll have good child-bearing hips." In the dressing room mirror I could see us from three different angles: my tall body and her tiny slim hands on it, how her smallness made me seem even larger. I made it a point never to be naked in front of her again. So even though the heat was making my skin itch under my clothes, even though I could taste salt on my upper lip, I stayed with Bridget on the side of the pool while my mother dove in, her naked body moving under the water like a silver minnow in a tide pool. When her head finally broke the surface, she saw me watching her and said, "Wow, it's colder in here than it looks. Sure you won't change your mind?"

I thought about begging her to get out of the water. All I could think about were those boys, who were probably still around here somewhere, or some lonely businessman on the third floor looking down from his window to find my mother in the pool in all her glory. I wanted to tell her to stop, and I had the feeling that she would if I asked her to—she was that worried about pleasing me—but I couldn't open my mouth. Admitting that her nakedness embarrassed me seemed like too cruel a thing to do. So instead I just sat there with my toes in the water and Bridget half-falling against my shoulder, watching my mother swim laps, her body so thin and graceful that she barely broke the water with her strokes, and thought about how, if I let them, things could always be this way: just my mother and my sister and me, with only the possibility of boys lurking in the shadows around us.

I said there was no way in hell I was sleeping with my mother, so she and Bridget shared one double bed and I got the other one all to myself. We slept late and in the morning we packed up and stopped for breakfast at a waffle place along the highway, and after that my mother said she wanted to see the caves.

It was a beautiful morning: not much humidity and the air that kind of clear piercing blue that's so clean it makes your lungs hurt a little when you breathe it in. Other than that, from what I could tell, West Virginia didn't look much different in the daylight from Ohio. In the restaurant, before she brought up the caves, my mother told us to order whatever we wanted, and for the first time since leaving home I felt really hungry. Even Bridget, obviously pukey from her hangover, managed to do some damage. I wondered if my mother had cleaned out my dad's accounts before we left, but then I closed my mind to that and thought instead about food, and about the way the boys in Florida might look: lean from swimming and bodysurfing, their bodies cooked brown by the sun. I should say that I hadn't changed my mind about this trip. I just had started thinking that it might be a good idea to see them down to Florida to make sure that Bridget arrived in one piece and that my mother didn't wander off with some man she'd met in a gift shop somewhere and forget all about her.

The caves were three hours south. After about an hour, my mother pulled off to the side of the road and tossed me the keys. "Forget it," I said. "I'm not contributing to this. I'm not going to help you run away."

But she was already undoing her seatbelt. "Please," she said, opening her door like she didn't notice the cars whizzing by her at eighty miles an hour. "I'm beat from yesterday. Give me a break, will you? Stop being such a baby."

I thought about refusing again, but she was already out of the car, standing with her back to the flying traffic like she thought she was protected by some invincible force field. In the driver's seat, I changed the radio to the only rock station I could find and promised myself that I would leave this part out when I told my father about the trip. How, while I drove and my mother dozed off in the backseat with Bridget, I could have turned the car around but didn't. How, driving, I almost felt good for a couple of minutes: free, excited, curious to see what was down the road. How, even though I was still as mad as ever, there was this small part of me that was caught up in it all and afraid to let my mother down.

We were at the caves by noon, and if my mother was relieved to see that I'd kept us on track, she didn't let on. She just stretched and said, "Wow, I must have needed that more than I thought." I watched in the rearview mirror as she woke Bridget, who was sleeping with her head tilted back and drool starting in one corner of her mouth. "Baby," my mother whispered, kissing her cheek. "Baby?"

"Cut it out," I said. "She's twelve."

I watched in the mirror as my mother sat back sharply. Bridget was awake by then. The three of us walked across the parking lot, the asphalt blistering in the noon sun, my mother pointing out all of the touristy crap I was trying to ignore: the life-sized wooden Indians, so old the paint on them was chipping; the other families posing for photographs by cardboard totem poles; the mini-golf course set off to one side of the parking lot, each hole partially concealed by a miniature cloth teepee. I'd expected the caves to be inside of a big mountain, but according to my mother's brochure they were underground, and could be entered only through the gift shop up ahead: a small log cabin with more totem poles on either side, looking like they were made out of plaster by fifth graders. My mother held Bridget's hand and said, "Isn't this great? Your father never would have let us stop here. Too important to make good time."

"This is crazy," I said. "I think I'll wait in the car."

She didn't look at me, but her smile tightened at the corners. She said, "You're too much like him. Can't you open your mind to an adventure?"

"Is that what this is?" I said, and laughed a little to show what I thought of it.

In the little cabin were rows of T-shirts and dream catchers and small plastic buckets full of geodes and feathers and arrowheads. While we waited in line at the cash register for the cave tour to begin, my mother leaned in and whispered, "You know, you were like this even as a baby. Always struggling, always pulling away."

I shrugged her off. Her breath tickled my ear.

"Why are you so angry?" she asked, and then sighed like she knew better than to wait for an answer. The line moved forward as the people in front of us paid for their tickets. Then she said, "If you think your father's so great, you should try being married to him sometime."

I looked around for Bridget, who was going through all of the bins of junk, sifting through polished gems and piles of fool's gold with her fingers. I saw her slip a couple of stones into her pocket and glance around to make sure no one was watching. I said, "We just want to go home."

"Go, then," my mother said. "No one's stopping you."

The tour was starting. People jostled and sidestepped to get to the front of the line, where a small woman named Tina was introducing herself before opening what looked like a closet door to reveal a dark wooden staircase that went down for what seemed like miles before disappearing into the blackness. Tina, the tour guide, lit a lantern then told everyone to stay together. "There are a few lights down below," she said loudly, "but be careful. Without them, you wouldn't be able to see your hand in front of your face." Bridget and my mother reached for each other. As we walked slowly down the staircase, the temperature got steadily cooler, and one of them, I'm not sure who, reached for my hand. I pulled away. All the way down, past the point that the darkness got so thick I could barely breathe, I could feel my mother there, a half-step behind, just waiting to touch me.

At the bottom, lanterns mounted on the damp walls lit the cave just enough that you could see the people closest to you, just enough to give you a sense that the caverns probably stretched for miles in either direction. It was cold down there too, the kind of cold that made it impossible to remember that it had ever been warm above ground. Tina was talking about the Indian tribes who had lived in the caves, which rooms they had used for meetings with the elders, or the narrow passageways where they hid from their enemies. She pointed to a large flat rock and said, "This is where they drew up their war plans." We all looked at the rock. It wasn't anything special, just a big flat rock, maybe the size of someone's kitchen table. Then Tina said she was going to show us what it felt like for the Indians down in that cave, and she cut the lights.

For a minute, I didn't know what was happening. For a minute I thought I had gone blind, the darkness was that complete. I could hear the voices of the rest of the group around me, mostly people laughing nervously, but I couldn't hear my mother. I put out my hands, backed up a step, and nearly tripped over a rock, my back scraping against the wall. In that moment of near panic, a voice inside me said: Okay, you have done it. You've disappeared. A couple of steps in any direction and I could be wandering for hours, even days, before anyone could find me. I thought about it, at least for a second. I thought how good it would feel to have her chase me for a change. Then, for no reason at all, a moment popped into my head, a picture from my childhood. My mother and I were in the shower together—I was maybe five—and she was shampooing my hair, and while she did it I was slapping her thighs with my small hands to make them jiggle; I liked the way that one little tiny bit of fat on her entire body could ripple that way, like a still pond that someone has just thrown a pebble into. Stop, she said a couple of times, but I didn't, and finally when she reached down and grabbed my hands, there were tears in her eyes. I was surprised at that: at how much I could hurt her, and how I hadn't only hurt her, I had felt good doing it. How it still felt good, how it would probably always feel good, these small cruelties, these little ways I had of causing her pain. I could do what I wanted to her and she would never stop me; maybe that's what real love is, this willingness to lay back and let people hurt you, and still give to them, just keep giving to them anyway.

In that second of panic, that instant before Tina turned the lights back on and in that small way saved us all, I didn't reach out, and I didn't move away. I stood still, listening to the sounds of strangers breathing all around me, with nothing to do while I waited for light but hold out hope of hearing something—anything—familiar.

Don Pomerantz
Zachariah Middleton
April Salzano
George Seli
William Miller
Brian Baumgart
Nils Michals
Thomas Alan Holmes
Steven Ray Smith
David Budbill
Simon Perchik
Sean McPherson

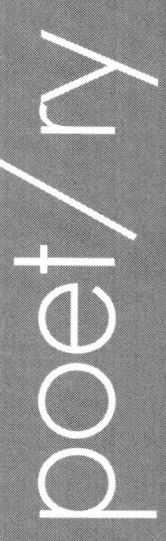

Shoes
Don Pomerantz

My shoes were afterthought and intimation, laces undone.
They touched the ground in ways I never knew.

My Feet: The Movie came too soon to a theater nearby
though they never walked on water or the emptiness
of space, passing out of the atmosphere,
what I was never able to say, or the land where
the dead and living embrace among leaves, so-called words
and uncountable chairs creaking and rocking.

The marked travelers lost, eating their shoes, feeding bellies
of desperation with worn out leather, what was gained?
Holding inside the weeks of arctic permafrost, Amazon
mud on fire, limbos of ecstasy, briefly everlasting.

Before my boots pointed suddenly upward,
God was a mini-bullet who spiraled through my chest
on his way to another unfinished friend.
The new technology proclaimed its dominion,
sweet moment of my Antietam, new nation ready
to tread another footprint upon its blossom
after stained blossom of uncountable skins.

Skin, skins, press yours now to mine, named or nameless,
with more wildflower meadows than forgetting, barefoot
or in heels that will not come undone on cobblestones,
washed out curbsides beyond repair or mulberries, red,
crushed, and littering the dumbstruck ground.

Niños Perdidos
Zachariah Middleton

With cherry juice staining his gums,
my little friend Hector threw his arms into the air, saying
I am nothing! I am the sky!

I looked around bewildered,
but before I could find a thought, I was dodging
a cherry thrown straight at my face.

I'm coming back to the farm
with a piece of embossed paper
that seems worth it's weight in timothy hay
and she's seventeen in three weeks.

Mischief under the covers
of the leaves is still mischief,
says my boss. My argument
is not based on disagreement.

Rather it exists in the days
when my brain swims
and my body walks
down to the river
and my hands are shaking
before my morning coffee.

2004 Saturn Vue
April Salzano

It was the one
I didn't want and the one I got
in the divorce. By then
it was nearly paid off, significantly
depreciated. There is nothing sadder
than measuring the length of a marriage
in interest and financing.
Black, my first

V6 engine, factory CD player,
and hell in the rain and snow. A sled
on four wheels, made of plastic. I rode it
down every slippery slope. Gradients
as high as speed bumps
caused loss of traction. I shit myself

in that car, another first, late
in a long line of premiers.
Not without regret, I traded it in, detailed
out the grease stains, kidprints and stickers
removed from the windows. So many journeys
becoming an anonymous odometer reading
on its final trip to the junkyard.

Making Figures in the Ward
George Seli

One cranes his neck
above his numbered state to see
a long line of prefigured men
inscribed on the whiteness of life—
sheets, pillowcases, and hallways—
with fading ink.

Their movements are timid estimates.
Their current positions are constants:
Limbs raised lowered stretched bent—
semaphore for incremental pain,
guiding in needle-thin jets
carrying Morpheus' visionaries.
An open-mouth cipher signals
breath encroached by null.

While some bodies convalesce,
others are leaning dance partners
with decay. And eyesight lasts
upon an aluminum medicine tray
until it's taken away
by little steps stuffed with carpet—
mysterious, like the steps to recovery.
Is that where one

Heads, lost to a realm of cotton fibrils,
dreamy inertia? Here, climate-controlled winds
never bend stiff reeds of gauze or undo
a baby-blue bib, but outlast a lord who
blew out something softly consonant with his fate.
Some protector.

Occasionally, faces poke through the curtain
at the realm's edge. Barely recognized,
they'll ask if one remembers A, B, C,
if one realizes the importance of X, Y, Z,
if the fingers raised are 1, 2, 3…

To have weak smiles and
no answers.

To have one's last moments
mottled by spots of light,
puppeted by a familiar unknown.

The House Where Jack Died
William Miller

I used to park outside it,
read scenes from *On the Road*,
Dharma Bums, one or two
of his final poems.

It was an ugly red house:
tacky, suburban, with a big
Florida room, dwarf palms
in the front yard.

He bought it for Stella,
his last wife, the one
who would get him sober,
back to writing books again.

But he still drank, palmed
beers from the fridge,
filled an aspirin bottle
with bourbon, sipped all day.

Then one morning he threw
up blood, kept throwing
it up, unable to stop even
when the ambulance came.

All the bags of blood
they dripped didn't stop
a common drunkard's death—
veins burst by a ruined liver…

So why did I go there if I
wanted to remember another
Jack, the eternal hitchhiker
between coasts?

I did it because he died
there, the man who wrote
the book before I was born
that opened up my own

endless road: New York,
Dublin, as far south as
New Orleans, real jazz
bands on St. Peter Street.

That road led to even these
quiet mornings, a poem,
a prayer, a favorite passage
read out loud.

Driving away, I always
looked back as if he might
be standing in the big
window, drunk, dying,

but still dreaming of all
those smoky Village clubs,
cool nights beneath
a thousand Denver stars.

Alex Tells Me He's Going to Every Powwow in the Midwest
Brian Baumgart

because he wants to be Indian
with black braids and feathers and alcohol and I
tell him that's not the way it is anymore or ever
was, though the boys I grew up with, including Alex,
acted the Indians out with those feathers and arrows,
but the alcohol wasn't until high school and by then
we'd forgotten Indians except the idea that we'd stolen
their lands somehow when we were asleep or not
yet born. Still, Alex says he enjoys the powwow,
the dance and music—thrumming
drums and chants, something else
shaking in the Black Hills of South Dakota
between sunset and sunrise, blurred,
he tells me, in visions he has, and I laugh
because his visions are stupors, and I
tell him so, but I'm wrong. The fires call louder
than a police siren, he says, and I believe
Alex would know after he spent the night
in jail outside Duluth last August and then again
in Des Moines, not at a powwow or dance but
drunk in public, according to the official
report Alex copied and showed to us like an award or badge
of service to alcoholics all around, though now he says
it's no good without the powwow because they got
fry bread and the Des Moines P.D. never did. After
a few beers he's a new man, an Indian or Native. To what?
I ask, but he's gone with black braids to Michigan,
the next powwow, the Great Dance.

On the News I Am to Be a Father
Nils Michals

1.
Pieces of the bottlebrush
tree blown indoors: faint red
line otherwise
missed.

2.
In which the books she reads on the sun
porch require more
of her turned
toward the condominium
pool—
                       look,
on her finger cut to such
mathematical stillness,
a topaz.

3.
Hopeless, the reverse geographies of hands:
whether the palm or the other,
the respective valleys therein,
that I must perfect
the required patience of the labors
there to come.

4.
Somewhere, a
fire.

5.
And then, on this, the first hot day, here come
the college kids in their lychee-
flavored bikinis, fists stuffed
with silver tallboys and neon
inflatables.
                          So goes
our cool square of blue
thought so essential to the pleasure
of certain books.

6.
Evening's remaining volley
of electrics, rain rising
out the trees, her just-washed
hair in lush passes; what it must
be to carve a small and pretty
thing to reside within, an old
key made of brass,
the dark of the lost lock
it fits within.

7.
Who can move more seductively to the *Law
& Order* theme song
than I? Of this, I am reasonably
certain: no one
else would
want to.

8.
The trace of grammar in concert with her body,
as in, I have been told, *fewer
not less*, as in, *further
not farther*, as in how
at certain inclinations of her neck when her hair's
put up
fall mispronunciations —
floating seeds
into the open mouths of those who love
too much the sound
of their own voice.

9.
The size of a sesame seed, building a heart.

10.
I'll be a long villa with every door thrown open.
Whatever's torn free—

                    feather, thread of silk, lottery
                    ticket, light—

I'll let pass across my tile
in its own time. *For what,*
you'll say. *Why*
not, I'll say.

Blue Bags
Thomas Alan Holmes

Three miles from route two, gravel spills
into a weed-choked ditch.
I bushhogged here two weeks ago,
touching up as I drove back
from checking Pawpaw's home.
I try the locks, secure loose window
clasps, look for broken panes.
I go into his house just long enough
to look for mice. My picture
on his console television
must be twenty years old.
I leave his porch light on.

But upstream from the highway,
in the ditch I find blue plastic
Walmart bags caught in the weeds—
sunblanched until "Live better"
fades almost completely out.
I wad the bags and pitch
them to my floorboard.

Two years ago, the old man saw
a bear cub in a treetop.
After two days, it fell—
only a loose tarpaulin.
"Wet hay and mice," he said.

Grand Jeté
Steven Ray Smith

Misha is suspended in midair—
Coppélia, 1978—
but not in a photo; he is still there—
the ne plus ultra of his grand jeté.

Friday nights we enter a champagne cocoon.
The children run in and out, in their teens,
while we hold stemware from our honeymoon.
They stop to brainstorm costumes for Halloween.

Whether Misha came down and his bones
joined those of other sixty-somethings is
the same as asking if we will be alone,
stalled in some mid-sentence without the kids.

When in doubt, go to Lincoln Center.
Look toward the top of the proscenium arch.
In grand ballon above the young who enter
the stage for their first Tchaikovsky march

Misha is there—today, yesterday—
just like we will be in these chairs
laughing at what you said on your way
out, and when you come back in from there.

Shucking Corn
David Budbill

I was shucking corn this evening,
      about 6:30,
a gentle evening light, the air still,
      temperature
dropping. Tonight, they say, it's
      going to be
in the forties, yet it's still early August.
      The beauty
of this evening is almost too much to bear,
      almost.
And, maybe because of that, I wonder
      how many
more summers I'll sit here shucking corn
      about 6:30
in the evening, in the still air, this gentle
      evening light.

*
Simon Perchik

Depending on the height, dust
is colder in the morning
though once you tuck the rag

it's the shelf that staggers
pulls you closer and slowly
smothered by something damp

made from lips, shoulders
and the invisible breathing
into pieces, smaller and smaller

till the air around your heart
won't let go this wood
no longer days or falling.

Take off the Leash
Sean McPherson

Take off the leash
And I'll float up
To the western wing
Of our attic

I'll turn pages under
Mossy shingles and
Snooze early
Beside the sea

Set me free
And I'll calmly converse
With dark seals
Barking phrasal verbs

My dreams of Zembla
Will earn my harp
A new string
In its lower register

My laziness
Will lend me the
Curious appeal
Of the sloth

Let me go away
And you'll soon read
Of my non-antics
In the papers

Mirth and pride
Will mark your cheeks
And you'll realize
You don't regret it

bio.graph.ies

Vol. 2, No. 1
Contributors

Cover Artist

Ivan de Monbrison was born in Paris in 1969. His work has appeared in *NY Arts Magazine*, *Anobium*, and elsewhere. His pieces have been shown internationally, at galleries including *Espace42*, the *Siena Art Institute*, and *Galerie du Croissant*. You can find sample artworks online at: http://artmajeur.com/blackowl

Poets & Writers

Jonathan Alston was born and raised in Northern California. He did beginning writing, or reading for that matter, until the of age twenty, when his new wife exposed him to written language. Now, writing is his life.

Brian Baumgart teaches in and directs the Creative Writing program at North Hennepin Community College, bordering Minneapolis, Minnesota. He holds an MFA from Minnesota State University, Mankato, and his writing has been published in various journals, including *Sweet*, *Ruminate*, *Blue Earth Review*, and *Diverse Voices Quarterly*.

J. D. Blair developed a thirty-year career in journalism and television production as a Writer and Producer. He was nominated twice for Emmy Awards for writing and producing documentaries and in 1998 was a awarded a Chris Award at the Columbus Film and Video Festival and was recipient of a Telly Award in 1999 for writing and producing the statewide program *California Heartland*. During this same period he was awarded a Knight Journalism Fellowship at the University of California, Berkeley for media coverage of urban development. Since 2000 he's been writing one-act plays, short fiction, essays and poetry.

Copper Canyon Press published **David Budbill**'s next to latest book of poems, *Happy Life*, in August 2011. It was on the poetry.org best seller list for 29 weeks. Exterminating Angel Press published his latest book of poems, *Park Songs: a Poem/Play*, in September 2012. His latest play, *A Song for My Father*, received two separate productions in 2010 and will be produced at The Western Stage in Salinas, CA, in 2013. Garrison Keillor reads frequently from David's poems on NPR's *The Writer's Almanac*. David lives in the southwest corner of Vermont's Northeast Kingdom. His website is at: http://www.davidbudbill.com/

Donald Budge is a writer who won the 2010 Blue Mesa Fiction Contest and has been published in *Prime Mincer*, *You're Going to Die*, and other places that are good. In 24 years, he has lost only one game of battleship, and came in second and third in arm wrestling tournaments before breaking his own arm at his arch enemy's birthday party.

Justin Campbell is a Biola University graduate and is currently a Graduate Teaching Fellow studying Creative Writing and Literature at Loyola Marymount University in Westchester, CA. His work deals mainly with issues of identity. He's currently working on a collection of short stories (and possibly a novel). He's been married to his beautiful wife, (and creative muse) Kaitlyn for just over a year and a half now.

William Cass has had thirty-eight short stories accepted for publication in mostly smaller literary magazines and anthologies. He lives and works as an educator in San Diego, California.

Valerie Cumming is a freelance writer, teacher, and editor based in Columbus, Ohio, where she lives with her husband and four daughters.

Robert Dart grew up in Vienna, Virginia, and has practiced law in Chicago and Los Angeles. He enjoys camping, the cinema, and going to bars. His novella, *Professional Responsibility*, is available for sale on Amazon and through other preferred dealers.

Tara Deal is a writer and editor in New York City and the author of two books from small presses: *Wander Luster* is a poetry chapbook from Finishing Line Press, and *Palms Are Not Trees After All* is the winner of the 2007 Clay Reynolds Novella Prize from Texas Review Press. Her writings have appeared in magazines such as *Blip*, *failbetter*, *Fogged Clarity*, *Opium*, *Sugar House Review*, and *West Branch*, among others. And her shortest story can be found in *Hint Fiction* (Norton). Visit her online at www.taradeal.com.

April Rosemary Ehrlich used to hate her middle name, but has learned to appreciate it because it reminds her of her grandma. She studied journalism and literature and is currently working on a community project that repairs the homes of senior citizens.

Patrick Falconi is a short story writer from Washington DC. He earned an undergraduate degree from VCU and an MFA from the American Film Institute Conservatory. His most recent writing credits include: "Freight," published by *OneTitle Reviews*, "Apropos of R. Brinkley Peabody," published by *A Clean, Well-Lighted Place*, "Genderflection," published by *Literary Orphans*, and "Yavenka and the Marigolds," published by *The Missing Slate*.

Thomas Alan Holmes, a member of the East Tennessee State University English faculty, lives and writes in Johnson City, Tennessee. Some of his work has appeared in *Louisiana Literature, The Appalachian Journal, Seminary Ridge Review, The Florida Review, Blue Mesa Review, The Black Warrior Review,* and *The Southern Poetry Anthology Volume III: Contemporary Appalachia,* with work forthcoming in *Cape Rock Journal, Stoneboat, The Connecticut Review, Iodine, Emerge,* and *The Noctua Review.*

Sean McPherson was born in Anchorage, AK, and currently resides in Olympia, WA. This spring he received his MA in Spanish and Portuguese from Tulane University. His poetry has appeared or is forthcoming in *The Bacon Review, The Commonline Journal,* and *Thirteen Myna Birds.*

Nils Michals is the author of *Lure,* which won the Lena-Miles Wever Todd award and was published by Pleiades and LSU Press in 2004. Individual poems have recently been published or are forthcoming in *diode, White Whale Review,* and *Bombay Gin.* An article, "The Metaphysical Object: Rilke and Image in Letters on Cezanne," recently appeared in *AboutaWord.* He currently lives in Boulder and is guest lecturer at the University of Colorado.

Zachariah Middleton is a cook at a food cart in Newberg, Oregon. He will graduate from George Fox University with his BA in Writing & Literature in the Spring of 2013. His poetry has been featured in *Pilgrimage Magazine, Chaffey Review, BROWN GOD, Cartographer Literary Review,* and others.

William Miller had published five collections of poetry, twelve books for chilldren and a mystery novel. He has recently published poems in *The Southern Review*, *Shehandoah* and *Prairie Schooner*. He lives and writes in the French Quarter of New Orleans.

Adam Padgett's fiction has recently appeared in *Appalachian Heritage* and *SmokeLong Quarterly* and has earned finalist positions in *Glimmer Train* fiction competitions and other contests. He currently resides in Charlotte, NC.

Simon Perchik is an attorney whose poems have appeared in *Partisan Review*, *The Nation*, *The New Yorker*, and elsewhere. For more information, including free e-books, his essay titled "Magic, Illusion and Other Realities," and a complete bibliography, please visit his website at www.simonperchik.com.

After much time in Western New England, **Don Pomerantz** now lives in New York City where he is a teacher. His poems have appeared in *Washington Square Review*, *Failbetter*, *Potomac Review*, *Eclectica*, *New Plains Review*, *Euphony*, and elsewhere.

April Salzano teaches college writing in Pennsylvania and is working on her first several collections of poetry and an autobiographical novel on raising a child with Autism. Her work has appeared in *Poetry Salzburg*, *Pyrokinection*, *Convergence*, *Ascent Aspirations*, *The Rainbow Rose*, *The Camel Saloon*, *The Applicant*, *The Mindful Word*, *Napalm and Novocain*, *Jellyfish Whispers*, *The South Townsville Micro Poetry Journal*, *The Weekender Magazine*, *Deadsnakes*, *Winemop*, *Daily Love*, *WIZ*, and is forthcoming in *Inclement*, *Poetry Quarterly*, *Decompression*, *Work to a Calm*, and *Windmills*.

Nicolas Sansone holds an MFA in fiction from the University of Massachusetts-Amherst and is the author of the novels *Shooting Angels* and *The Calamari Kleptocracy*. His short fiction has appeared in a number of venues, including *PANK*, *Pear Noir!*, *Bartleby Snopes*, *NANO Fiction*, *Denver Syntax*, *Word Riot*, and *The Los Angeles Review*. For more information, visit his website at http://nicksansone.yolasite.com.

George Seli is a New York-based trade magazine editor and doctoral candidate in philosophy. His poetry has appeared in several journals, including *Crab Creek Review*, *Epicenter*, and *Steam Ticket*.

Ashley Sgro has always been infatuated with words and writing. As an avid reader and eternal writer, she dedicates her free time to composing poetry and flash fiction. Ashley currently lives with her family in New Jersey and can be visited at ashleysgro.com.

Steven Ray Smith's poems have appeared in *The Kenyon Review*, *The Raintown Review*, *Garbanzo*, *Prick of the Spindle*, *Bayou*, *The Broken Plate*, *Poetry South*, *Stepaway Magazine*, *Skidrow Penthouse*, *Dogs Singing—A Tribute Anthology from Salmon Poetry of Ireland*, and others. New work is forthcoming in *GRAIN*, *American Antheneaum*, *The Lindenwood Review*, *Common Ground Review*, *The Cape Rock*, *Big Muddy*, *Writer's Bloc*, *Slant*, and *riverrun*. He is the president of a culinary school and lives in Austin with his wife and children.

D. Z. Watt used to live in the US but moved to Scotland more than a decade ago. In the US he had many poems and texts published in the 1980s zine scene, and more recently has had fiction in *Flash: The International Short-Short Fiction Magazine*, *The Ranfurly Review*, and *Kerouac's Dog*, with more to come in *BareBack* and other places. His published fiction blog is at http://dzdubya.blogspot.com/

Kirby Wright is the author of the companion novels *Punahou Blues* and *Moloka'i Nui Ahina*, both set in the islands.

Shellie Zacharia lives in Florida. Her work has appeared in *The Pinch*, *Sou'wester*, *Opium*, *Weave*, *A cappella Zoo*, and elsewhere. She is the author of the story collection *Now Playing* (Keyhole Press, 2009).

Editors

Tristan Beach is a native of Washington State. He has a BA in English from Saint Martin's University and is currently pursuing an MFA at Goddard College. He has held internships at Copper Canyon Press and Coffee House Press. His reviews have appeared in *The Conium Review* and *Cutbank*, and his poetry has appeared in *Pitkin Review*. He enjoys film noir, jazz, racy poetry, and coffee art.

James R. Gapinski's writing has appeared in such publications as *Line Zero*, *Pudding Magazine*, *Burdock Magazine*, *Oak Bend Review*, and *Calliope Nerve*. James is an MFA candidate at Goddard College, he currently serves as Editor In Chief of the *Pitkin Review*, and he teaches a short story writing course at Mt. Hood Community College. He lives in Portland, Oregon with his partner and the obligatory two cats required of every generic bio.

Susan Lynch is primarily a poet whose works have been published in *ASH* (the Oxford Poetry Society's quarterly magazine), *Enizagam*, *Poetry Space*, and *Calliope Nerve*. A published songwriter since the 80's, Joan Jett's cover of her song (with Larry Whitman) "My Big Reward" appears on the soundtrack of Nora Ephron's film, *Lucky Numbers*. She teaches, writes and teaches writing, poetics, and is designing the Romantic Poetry Elective Course for *Shmoop* among other projects. She holds a BA in English from Reed College, studied literature at Oxford University, and this summer completes the MFA degree in Creative Writing from Goddard College.

Uma Sankaram holds an MA in Forensic Psychology from John Jay College in New York, an MS in Clinical Psychology from Pacific University, and is a doctoral candidate at Pacific University. Along with other Conium Press editors, Uma co-hosts the "Somethingesque Reading Series" in Portland, Oregon. Uma appreciates the written word, even though her own communication abilities are mostly limited to squeaks, growls, and other random noises.

Marc Schuster is the author of *The Grievers* (The Permanent Press, 2012) and *The Singular Exploits of Wonder Mom and Party Girl* (The Permanent Press, 2011). He is the editor of *Small Press Reviews* and a contributing editor for *Shelf Unbound*. He also teaches writing and literature courses at Montgomery County Community College in Blue Bell, Pennsylvania.

Holly Tri has a BAS in Psychology from the University of Minnesota Duluth and a MFA in Creative Writing from Goddard College. She recently moved with her family from Minnesota to Oregon. Holly writes fiction and has a passion for ancient and medieval history.

Made in the USA
Charleston, SC
23 January 2013